MEMORIES OF OTHER WORLDS?

She was the sole inhabitant of that isolated planetoid, but when she looked out at the frozen vastness of the sky she could gaze at a blue sun and think of the Chidnim who basked in its warmth, at an orange one and picture the Tansils at play, overhead at a pure white one and remind herself that was the orb shining on the cities of the Tark.

Catching sight of her reflection in a polished dial, she spent a brief moment admiring her pure green complexion, the symmetrical patterns of the scales on her face, the litheness of her neck and arms. A modicum of reassurance was always welcome. . . .

But it wouldn't be when she woke up —because *she* was actually in a modern house in a modern Earthly city— and the memories that were so clear were utterly impossible—unless they were the suppressed memories of an alien in hiding.

John Brunner

GIVE WARNING TO THE WORLD

DAW BOOKS, INC.

DONALD A. WOLLHEIM, PUBLISHER

1301 Avenue of the Americas
New York, N. Y.   10019

Published by
THE NEW AMERICAN LIBRARY
OF CANADA LIMITED

Cover art by Jack Gaughan.

John Brunner novels in DAW Books:

THE STARDROPPERS	UQ1023
ENTRY TO ELSEWHEN	UQ1026
FROM THIS DAY FORWARD	UQ1072
THE WRONG END OF TIME	UQ1061
POLYMATH	UQ1089

First Printing, July, 1974

1 2 3 4 5 6 7 8 9

PRINTED IN CANADA
COVER PRINTED IN U.S.A.

 I

Traffic drone punctuated by the sound of occasional impatient car horns. Sunlight, slanting between ill-drawn curtains. Hunched in a fetal posture under the one sheet which was all she could bear over her in this hot weather, Sally Ercott woke from terror to terror.

Her throat was sore, as though she had been screaming in her sleep. But if she had, the screams must have been silent. No one had come to see what was the matter with her. . . .

Like the dying chime of a bell, her mind rang with the echo of such nightmare that on realizing she was still here, still in this squalid horrible house, she could not prevent herself from bursting into tears.

The pillowcase, like the bedsheets, was ever so slightly greasy, as though the cloth were so old it could never again be washed wholly clean, as though that same smear of barely perceptible grime which made the floral wallpaper of this gloomy room repulsive to the touch had permeated the material and made it forever clammy, like damp leather.

Nonetheless she buried her face in it, racked with sobs.

It was always like this on waking. Instead of escaping from the terrible trap of her dreams into a wholesome normal ordinary world, she moved into another and infinitely more fearful prison. Something abominable, something unspeakably foul, loomed in her awareness. It was as though pure cruelty could be

5

distilled into a dark hideous cloud. It haunted her at the corner of vision, never quite being there when she tried to confront it directly, yet never going away.

Eventually she was able to master her misery. Her next—automatic—reaction was to look at her left wrist. Her watch wasn't there, of course. It was at the pawnbroker's in Praed Street, and had been since the last time she managed to leave the house. How long ago? More than a week.

But judging by the traffic noise, and the angle of the sunlight on the wall which never reached this room's window until the morning was far advanced because there was a high-rise apartment block diagonally opposite, it must be nearly noon. She shuddered, her whole slim body convulsed by a spasm of nausea.

Oh, Christ. What did I do to deserve this living hell?

For a while longer she lay incapable of moving. Then, overhead, a clattering noise announced the departure of Mrs. Ramsay on her Saturday trip all the way from the attic to the street with her overflowing bucketful of garbage. She was elderly and arthritic and it always took her ages to complete the journey even when she didn't spill half her load and have to break off and pick it up.

It would be intolerable to wait out that inexorable thud, thud, thud until it climaxed in a triumphant clash of dustbin lids. Angrily, hating herself without knowing why, Sally Ercott swung her feet to the floor.

The phone beside Nick Jenkins' bed rang shrilly. Rolling over, reaching by reflex for his glasses and thrusting them into place, he clutched the receiver with his other hand.

"Yes?"

"You old slugabed," rumbled a familiar voice. "Never tell me I woke you up!"

Nick stretched to his full length, which was considerable. He was a tall lean young man with tousled brown hair, a thin sharp-chinned face, his lifelong myopia lending him a somewhat absentminded air except when he donned his glasses, whereupon he looked what he was: scholarly and talented.

"Oh, it's you, Tom," he muttered. "I haven't forgotten our lunch date, if that's what you rang up about." Rising on one elbow, he glanced at his alarm clock. "And what's more I'm not late. We said one o'clock, and here it is only a quarter to twelve."

"Knowing what you're like on a Saturday," Tom Gospell said caustically, "I though I'd better make sure you were in plenty of time. Particularly since that old banger of yours is liable to break down if someone gives it a dirty look."

"It is not an old banger! It's a classic XK120 and it's one of the best sports cars ever built!"

"Hmm! I did wake you, didn't I? No need to be snappy, you know. All right, see you at one sharp. And since it's such a fine day, if you have nothing fixed for afterward, I'll give you the chance to convince me you're right about the Jag. Give me a ride to some place where we can enjoy the sunshine. It's a lovely day, and I don't have to meet Gemma until six."

"It's a deal," Nick said around a yawn.

Chief Inspector Bill Dougherty turned the key he had drawn this morning at Scotland Yard and entered one of the eleventh-floor apartments in the tall block overlooking Mamble Row. On the way along the corridor from the elevators, two or three of the residents had favored him with suspicious scowls. Maybe the cover story wasn't going to stand up much longer.

Which will please the Borough Council, of course. Lord, the rigmarole we had to go through to persuade them to leave this place empty with four hundred families on their waiting list for new accommodation! And we did expect to be out in three weeks, not over six. . . . . I thought this flat was a godsend. Lately it's been feeling more like a millstone.

The rooms were bare, echoing, stark, devoid of furniture or carpets, although naturally the windows were curtained. In the main living room they stayed drawn virtually all day. That was going to attract attention, sooner or later.

Just so long as it's not so soon the operation goes bust.

At the window of the living room a young constable in plain clothes was on watch. Seated in a stackable plastic chair, he was gazing through a pair of high-power binoculars on a tripod stand. At his left a phone and a tape recorder reposed on a small folding table. Also on a tripod, a camera with a telephoto lens stood at his right, permanently focused on Number 5 Mamble Row. There was nothing else in the room bar the remains of a snack breakfast, an empty paper cup, and a disposable plate with the crust of a sandwich lying on it.

And a lot of dust.

"Morning, Hedger," Dougherty said, closing the door.

The constable started. "Morning, sir!" he exclaimed. "I didn't hear you come in. If I may say so, you have a hell of a light tread for—uh . . ."

"For such a fat man?"

Hedger looked injured. "I was going to say *heavy*, sir."

"That too." Dougherty sighed. "Runs in the family, I'm afraid I often marvel at the fact that I don't make whole buildings shake. . . . Anything interesting I haven't heard?"

"No, this watch has been pretty uneventful. You heard that Dr. Argyle called again last night—yes? I got a picture of his car, though I'm not sure there was enough light to show the figures on the license plate. And of course I logged Mrs. Rowall out and back as usual."

"Did she bring anybody with her?"

"No, she came back alone."

"Mm-hm." Dougherty rubbed his clean-shaven chin. "Mind if I take a quick squinch?"

"Uh . . ." Hedger, for some reason, was perceptibly

embarrassed. But he relinquished his chair and stood aside dutifully.

Eyes to the binoculars, Dougherty uttered a sound halfway between a chuckle and a snort.

"Any special reason, apart from the fact that she's pretty and sleeps with nothing on, for you to have these glasses focused on the window of the girl's room?"

Hedger, who was very young, blushed vivid pink.

"Yes, sir!"

"What?" Dougherty murmured, adjusting the binoculars to show the front entrance of the house instead of the next-to-top windows.

"Well—ah—it's only since that time she fell down the front steps that Argyle's been calling, right?"

"Go on."

"And one knows about Argyle, how close he came to jail for over-prescribing hard drugs, and one knows that Bella Rowall is one of the most notorious tarts in Soho. . . . I was talking things over with Bob Prior last night when he came to relieve me, and it seems he's come to the same conclusion I have."

"I'm still listening," Daugherty said, adjusting the glasses a second time so that they swept the whole of the narrow decaying street called Mamble Row.

"Well, sir," Hedger said, swallowing, "any time we like we could knock off this character Alfred Rowall for living on immoral earnings. It hasn't been done. That implies that the real essence of the case must be a lot bigger. Now Dr. Argyle keeps dropping around at unlikely hours, so . . . well, it hangs together logically, doesn't it?"

Dougherty rose from the chair with some effort; he was, as Hedger had remarked, a very heavyset man, going bald and with large dark bags under his eyes, testimony to years of insufficient sleep.

"I'm not going to give you a straight answer," he haid. "Sorry, but I don't make Squad policy, you know. That's done at the very top, up at Commander level. But I will say this: I think you did the right thing when you opted for CID. Keep up the brainwork and

do a bit more background research. Take my advice
and you'll make sergeant one of these days."

Grinning, he clapped Hedger on the shoulder and
headed for the door.

"Morning, Mrs. Ramsay," Clyde West said as he
ascended the stairs carrying his Saturday bag of
groceries. He stood back on the landing to let her
pass with her garbage, and received as reward an
answering grunt. She had no breath to spare for friendly
chat.

Today his bag was even lighter than usual. It was
going to be tough spinning out the supplies until next
weekend. But there were, after all, people worse off
than him.

In fact there was one right in this house.

*Maybe I should ask if she'd like something? She
never seems to get a square meal. . . .*

Passing Sally Ercott's door on the way to his, he
made to knock at it, checked, looked for a long
moment at the dark brown back of his hand, and concluded for the tenth time that if Sally wanted help she
could come out and ask for it. They'd been living in
the same house for weeks and she'd hardly exchanged
a civil word with him. Let the Rowalls do the worrying.

Shrugging, he went into his own room and shut the
door.

II

Staggering a little as she rose from bed, Sally had to rest one hand on the back of the room's solitary armchair. Its seat cushion was torn and oozed sour flock; moreover the back of it was almost slimy with hair oil left by lodgers long ago when it was fashionable for men to slick down their hair.

She caught sight of herself in the full-length mirror on the door of the wardrobe, which lacked a leg and was kept level by half a brick. Wanting very much to ignore the image of the state she was in, she compelled herself to look by a supreme effort of will.

Except for panties she was naked . . . and those were stained. Her shoulder-long blonde hair was tangled and kept falling over her blue eyes. When she brushed it aside she noticed the back of her hand was dark with grime.

Still she went on staring, as though she imagined that loathing could do what other of her emotions could not.

Can that hair be mine—rat-tailed, knotted, overdue for a shampoo since God knows when? Can those be my eyes, red with weeping between swollen puffy lids? Can that be my mouth, chapped and sore? Can that dirty body be mine, with all those marks across it from creases in the bedsheet?

She looked from the reflection to the actuality, raising her arms, gray detached separate things not belonging to the real Sally. On the unwashed skin, a brown

11

mark associated with an underlying tenderness. She
rubbed the spot. There was a tiny prick there and it
had bled a little. What in the—?

Oh, yes. Last night that doctor, sent for by the
Rowalls, had called again. A nasty man who wouldn't
listen even if she wept. Very suitable for a person like
Bella. Sally was in no doubt concerning what her landlady did for a living. This house were she and her husband Alfred rented out rooms must be no more than a
colorable excuse for them having an income. Who'd
believe, though, that such a near-slum would bring in
enough for two people to live on? She glanced around,
seeing the filthy-backed chair, the canted wardrobe, the
bed with its sagging spring where last night she had
slept so badly—until she fell into stupor—that she
ached now from head to foot, as though she had passed
hours fleeing in panic from some unspeakable horror. . . .

All of a sudden she wanted to get out of here. Automatically she reached for her clothes, tossed anyhow
on the seat of the armchair: a bra, a dress, a summer-
weight coat. Her shoes, scuffed and filthy, were lying
on the floor nearby. That was all. At first there had been
something more . . . hadn't there? Oh, yes: tights which
had shredded into holes long ago, and a purse which—

No good. She couldn't remember what had become
of her purse. Though she did know that what money
had been in it was all spent.

The touch and sight of her clothes, however, com-
pounded her revulsion. She stared at the first item, her
bra, as if she had never seen it before.

Christ, it can't belong to me! Not this foul rag!

Wildly she completed her inventory of the room,
wanting with all her might to spot something, anything,
that might reassure her about herself. The rug on the
floor—but it was trodden threadbare. There was a picture over the mantel, fly-specked and with cracked
glass, and anyhow it was hideous. At the window
faded curtains, by the bed a rickety occasional table,
screwed to the wall an empty shelf. Nothing else.

Nothing. Not a handkerchief, a paper tissue, a bar of soap, a comb. . . .

I've gone mad. Crazy. Out of my mind!

What other explanation could there be?

"But I don't want to be insane!" she moaned softly to the walls. "I don't, I don't, and I can't think why I should be!"

She closed her eyes, and for a tantalizing moment she imagined she was about to recall what she had—somehow—forgotten . . . but it leaked away, as though she had tried to catch and hold a single snowflake.

I am Sally Ercott. I am—I think—twenty-five years old. I come from—come from—come from . . .

Useless. No matter how she struggled she couldn't break down the barrier separating her from her past life. She tried a different tack.

When I passed this house and saw a sign up for a room to let I was on my way to—But I didn't want a room, I didn't need one, I had a home of my own and is that why somebody hid my purse in case I'd find some note in it of where my home was, where it IS?

A cry escaped her, but she stifled it from pure shame. She knew she had been seen filthy and ill-clad by the other lodgers; even so, she hated thinking about the fact. . . .

Sudden idea. Perhaps if I make myself more like the way I used to be, more presentable, something else will come back.

Aware all hope was fragile, but clinging to this one with all her might, she reasoned it out by careful stages.

There's a bathroom across the landing, even if I have no money for the gas meter so I shall have to make do with cold water. And I have no soap. Maybe I could ask Mrs. Ramsay for a bit, and even the loan of a comb? Or the Rowalls . . . ? No, I don't want to talk to the Rowalls, even though they have brought the doctor in for me and let me fall behind with the rent.

Images arose in her mind: Bella the blowsy dyed redhead, probably in her middle thirties but looking years older; her husband Alfred with receding dark hair and a receding chin and a voice that was halfway to a whine. . . .

I think the reason why they're being kind to me is that—well, they want to rope me into the same work Bella does. I mean if they were really friendly they'd give me food instead of . . .

She rubbed the prick-mark on her arm. It wasn't the first.

Overhead a door slammed and a clang followed as Mrs. Ramsay dumped her empty garbage pail in its usual place under the sink. With a start Sally realized she had brooded so long, she had missed her chance to confront the old lady and beg her help. Should she go up and knock on her door . . . ?

No. In this state she didn't want to enter anybody's home, even for a moment. She could imagine herself leaving behind a contaminating aura, a trace of the foulness darkening her mind.

Well, perhaps if I'm lucky someone will have forgotten a cake of soap in there. And even plain water might help.

Clutching her coat around her she scurried barefoot into the bathroom. And—yes! Providentially there was some soap on the handbasin. Only a sliver that the owner felt not worth keeping, but a gift from the gods to Sally Ercott.

Bolting the door, she hung up her coat and stepped out of her panties; they were of lightweight material and would dry in next to no time. Having washed them, she washed herself, all over. She made a vast wet mess on the linoleum. But what the hell?

And there was even a towel: the communal hand towel, overdue for laundering and tattered at the edges but usable. She had just flung it back on its hook, was donning her coat again, when horror overtook her.

It was as though a giant hand had reached through her ribs and clutched her heart. The room swam, the floor swayed. She fought to control herself. Like the aura felt by an epileptic or a migraine victim, a sense of foreboding invaded her mind. Struggling as long as she could, she concentrated on mundane things: arms into coat sleeves, buckle the belt, unbolt the door, and—

And without interval she was no longer here. No longer in London.

No longer, perhaps, anywhere.

In the downstairs front room, the Rowalls' living room, Bella said to her husband Alfred, "I'm on my way."

Laying aside the newspaper he'd been reading, he said nervously, "I'm not happy about the girl, you know."

"So what? You mean you can't cope?"

Hanging her raincoat—slick, wet-looking plastic—over her arm, his wife favored him with an ill-tempered glare. She was dressed in her working gear: a skimpy frock with a ridiculously low-cut neck and an extremely short skirt, and shoes with immensely high heels.

"What about her?" she rasped. "Come on—it's Saturday, you know, and I want to get down west."

"I . . ." Alfred licked his lips. "I don't know. But I have a bad feeling about her. Sort of a premonition."

"Then you can bloody well sort her out yourself," Bella snapped, and marched away.

Left alone, he pondered nervously for a while. Eventually he gathered his energy and went out into the hallway and turned toward the stairs. His eyes widened in alarm as he saw Sally emerge from the bathroom—but instead of returning to her own room, she came rushing down so fast it seemed she must fall.

She didn't. And when he tried to seize hold of her she eluded him as neatly as an eel and was out on the street before he could draw breath.

"Come back!" he shouted. "Come back!"

And when she didn't, all he could think of doing was shut the front door.

"I told her," he muttered. "She can't say I didn't warn her, can she?"

Down the irregular twisting pathways of the caverns that wove through the heart of the mountain lay the trail which had been taken by the man Iwys, the trail she too had chosen to follow. She was weary and her tender feet were blistered, but she kept on.

For the mid-part of the way there was no light, and she had to grope. Eventually, though, there was a sort of dull green luminescence, and the air grow full of a putrid stench. Then her heart almost failed her, and she thought of the advice given her by well-meaning friends:

"It is no use to mourn for Iwys now. We have seen many taken from us. We have seen thousands with that look of blind purpose in their eyes, who would not stay even to bid farewell. All have gone into the mountain. Not one has returned. True, it is a shame Iwys was taken, who meant so much to you. But it is known the creature who called him cares nothing for what we think or want."

"Then," she had exclaimed with wild grief, "if it cares nothing for what and who we are, let it take me instead of Iwys!"

And there, to her left, in the wider street which carried a lot of traffic . . . !

She screamed his name and rushed toward him: "Iwys! Iwys!"

At the wheel of an elderly open sports car, a young man with spectacles looked around in astonishment, nearly causing an accident as a red light changed to green and other drivers behind expected him to move forward.

A wild-haired, wild-eyed girl had jumped over the car's side, into the passenger seat, and was babbling an incomprehensible name and looking at him with such intensity he might have been her long-lost childhood sweetheart.

III

"What the hell do you think you're playing at?" Nick Jenkins barked. But he perforce drove on across the intersection in search of a place where he could legally stop and turn this crazy stranger out of his car.

Over and over she said, "Iwys, *Iwys.* . . ."

The end of this tunnel was closed by a kind of chitinous flap. She reached toward it with a trembling hand. Before she touched it, however, it fluttered around the edges, where it was rubbery and flexible to ensure a tight seal to the rock, then folded and drew aside.

Beyond was revealed a place full of green-white luminance, hurtful to her eyes after so long in darkness. In shape it was like a bag laid on its side. Everywhere, in warm fetid air, things like ferns waved and gestured.

Those, she realized with a pang of nausea, must be tendrils of the creature's substance. Accustomed all her life to looking outward at the world, she was revolted by the notion of a beast whose outward aspect was also its inward one; however, by a vast effort, she maintained her presence of mind.

A voice spoke, whisperingly, susurrantly, seeming to issue from everywhere at once. It made the flesh crawl on her bones. It said, "Come forward."

Somehow she found the resolution to comply. When she stepped past the entrance of the creature's body, her feet sang very slightly into softness, exactly as though she were walking on the flayed flesh of a dead animal. But this beast was not dead. Where the rocks had worn her sandals into holes she could feel the surface underfoot moist and warm.

She said, "I—I come. . . ." And choked on the words.

The creature's voice replied. "You come," it said affirmatively. "And yet you were not sent for."

"It is to ask you a favor. Take me in place of the man you claimed yesterday, my lover Iwys!"

She set her shoulders defiantly, feigning courage, trying not to stare at the waving fronds above, ahead, on either side. What a place of nightmare! As though one could walk down one's own gullet and watch intestines go about their business of digestion!

"It is all one to me which of you I have," said the creature. "So long as you are strong and in good health. I do not take account of the names you use, so I am unaware which of those I last summoned is called Iwys. In any case, however, you are too late. Look."

She put her hands to her mouth. She wished she could hide her eyes with them, but something forced her to watch what was happening. At the far side of the pouch-shaped enclosure a sphincter opened, and the greenish light grew brighter. Beyond, she could see . . .

People. But deformed. Hideously, horribly changed. Legs could still be discerned, arms too, but their heads—! Embedded in something slimy, glaucous, alien!

"I could not release them now," the creature said. "Not even if I chose to, which I do not. Moreover, since their brains have been emptied from their heads, were I to do so they would immediately die."

"But what do you want with them?" she cried, fighting tears.

"To spread my kind. You afford my children what they lack: strong limbs to carry them far and fast, then dig them burrows where they will be safe until maturity."

The sphincter oozed shut with a sucking sound.

"I have no present use for you," the creature said. "If you wish, I will kill you. Otherwise you can go. Next year perhaps I may choose you to carry one of my offspring. I think I shall. None of you ever came willingly to me before."

To have her brain "emptied" from her skull . . . ? No, no! There could be nothing more horrible, not even death!

"Kill me, then!" she shrieked, and launched herself in a fury of clawing hands at the nearest portion of the creature. Something that stank leaked out, the ichor of its existence. And next moment—

—it was as though she had been transported into yesterday.

Then was made up of adequate money, pretty clothes, boyfriends with cars, theaters, books, music. *Now* consisted of a squalid room in a dirty back-street near Paddington Station, the wheedling delusive kindness of the Rowalls, the brusque resentful attention of Dr. Argyle, the contempt she was sure she could read in the eyes of the West Indian who rented the room next to hers, and Mrs. Ramsay on the attic floor.

But—but . . .

Here she was in the passenger seat of an open Jaguar sports car, old but in beautiful condition. The sun was shining down and a lively pop song was emanating from the radio under the dashboard, and at the wheel sat a good-looking young man in an open-necked shirt and scarf, gazing at her through horn-rimmed glasses.

So this definitely must belong to *then* instead of *now!*

A second later, and she was overcome by horror and shame. Reality swept aside her moment of self-deception. She recalled that she was naked but for her coat, and barefoot into the bargain, and that she had rushed out of the street where she lodged, Mamble Row, and jumped into this car when it halted for a red light on the wider cross-street, shouting at the driver as though she knew him. But she didn't. And anyway, who had ever been called by a ridiculous name like "Iwys"?

Her face caught fire. Mumbling something, she turned to find the door handle and let herself out; by now, the driver had found a spot where he could pull up at the curb.

To her surprise and dismay, he said, "Not so fast!" And closed a steely grip on her wrist.

She struggled to break loose. The sleeve of her coat rode up her arm. Revealed was the prick-mark she had found on waking.

At once the young man's fingers let go.

"I see," he said in a dull voice. "Might have guessed. Go and make trouble for somebody else, hm? I have a date for lunch, *and* I don't like junkies!"

Bewildered, she paused with her hand on the door catch. "Junkie?" she echoed in a faint voice. "Me? *Me?* Oh, no! I swear not! I never took anything the doctor didn't give me—it was a doctor who gave me this injection, just last night!"

"I'm glad to hear it," the driver said, his expression softening a little. "Even so, given the way you came screaming at me and jumped in the car without a by-your-leave, I feel you ought to go right back to your doctor."

"Sally!" a sharp voice said from the curbside. "What in hell do you think you're playing at?"

Charging toward the car from a nearby bus stop, a woman about forty, medium-tall and medium-plump, in an extraordinary orange dress that clashed with her brilliant red hair, a slick black raincoat over her arm, and too much makeup.

At the sight of her the girl addressed as Sally shrank back, clasping her hands before her mouth.

"Ah . . ." It was all happening too fast for Nick to take in. He said, "You two know each other?"

"Know her?" the woman in the too-short dress grunted. "Oh yes. I'm sorry she's bothered you. Come on, Sally, I'll take you home."

"No," Sally said. *"No!"*

"Don't give me that." The older woman tore open the door. "Out with you!"

"Oh, please!" Sally turned beseechingly to Nick.

"Don't pretend you don't know me!" the woman barked. "Go on, tell him who I am!"

"She's—she's my landlady, but—"

"More than that," the woman broke in. "God knows why *I* have to be a soft touch, but I am, and I can't help it. Did we get the doctor for you when you fell ill? *Did* we—me and my husband Alfred?"

"Y-yes!" In a strangled tone, as though the lie would have been intolerable.

"All right, then! Come on out of there like I said. I'll see you back and send for the doctor again. Obviously the treatment isn't working too well." She caught Sally's arm, and this time the girl yielded. She went on, "Oh, look at you! No shoes, and—hell, nothing but your coat! Oh, you really *are* in a bad way, aren't you?" Putting her arm around Sally's shoulders. "But you'll be OK. Take it easy, just take it easy . . . . Sorry about all this, mister," she added to Nick. "She's no relation of ours, but we feel sort of responsible."

"I—" Nick began, but Bella had forcibly turned Sally away and was marching her back along the street the way she had come.

He sat staring after the two women for a minute or so, until an angry blast on the horn of a following car reminded him that he was stopped illegally, and he drove off to keep his date with Tom Gospell.

A few hundred yards later . . .

"You fool, you fool, you incompetent bastard!" shrieked Bella Rowall. "If my bus had been there one minute sooner . . . !"

Facing her in the hallway of their home, Alfred put

up his arms as though to ward off a blow. He said defensively, "I warned you the girl was—"

"And I told you to sort her out, and you didn't!" She kicked the front door shut behind her with a crash. She was no longer pretending to handle Sally gently. The grip she had on the girl's arm was tight as a vice. "You let her get out, didn't you? Christ, she must have walked straight past and you didn't stop her!"

"She didn't walk!" Alfred flared. "She ran in a blind panic, and when I tried to grab hold of her she—"

"I don't believe you even tried to catch her," Bella interrupted. "You're not only a fool, you're a coward too. Scared of a girl no stronger than a straw, half-starved and almost out of her mind!"

Regaining a scrap of her lost dignity, Alfred retorted, "When she ought to be *completely* out of it by now! And at the rate you and your precious chum Argyle are going, she never will be. She could be safely packed away in an asylum by now, if it weren't for your bloody *cautious approach!*" He made the last two words sound like an obscenity.

"It's got to be done right," Bella said. All the tension had suddenly vanished from her voice. "Because if it isn't, then we're dead, aren't we?"

Alfred gulped noisily and nodded.

"OK, so we do it my way. And let's hurry because if I'm not up west in an hour or so, this weekend's takings will go for a burton and we can't afford that. Help me drag her up the stairs and lock her in her room. She only has her coat on, and that's given me an idea. We'll leave her with nothing to wear at all. I can't see her running out in the street naked, can you?"

Alfred brightened. "That would be a perfect shortcut. They'd be bound to lock her up, and in a week or two she really would be crazy."

Bella's expression grew a fraction more cordial. "Hmm! Yes, provided they don't come around here asking awkward questions. . . . Ask Richard about it, right away. Call him up as soon as I've gone and keep on trying until I get back. And don't let her slip

through your fingers again, hear? Come on, you!"
Viciously twining her hand into Sally's greasy fair hair
as though taking a dog by its lead.

Docile, tears streaming down her face, Sally obeyed.

IV

So what the hell is it those bastards have against the girl?

Judging it politic to wait out any quarrel between his landlady and landlord, Clyde West had opened and then promptly shut his door. He counted himself lucky to have found a moderately cheap, moderately clean room in this house. It was very difficult for anybody to find rented accommodations in London these days, and if you happened to be black the problem was, as they said, redoubled in spades. He couldn't be choosy. He was, at least in theory, an actor, and in the cant phrase he was resting. More bluntly, he was out of work. As usual. Even in TV there were few openings for West Indians, while the stage was dominated by long-running plays and a couple of subsidized repertory companies. The result was that the best job he had landed in months was a walk-on bit in an airline commercial.

Depression had numbed his mind.

Even so . . .

He was aware of what was going on around him even though he would have preferred not to be, and his conscience was beginning to nag. He didn't give a fig for the way Bella Rowall made most of her money. Precisely because this lodging house was used as a cover story rather than to extract maximum profits from the tenants, he was benefiting. Elsewhere he might have been held to ransom for twice as much

24

per week. Though the place was sleazy, it was tolerable. Kicking up any kind of fuss would be cutting off his nose to spite his face.

But—but damn it! That snooty blonde girl in the next room who won't so much as smile at me! I think they're holding her prisoner!

There. It was clear in his mind: the horrible suspicion he hated before he formulated it, because it might imply the need to resume the lonely frustrating chore of apartment hunting.

He cast his mind back with determination, to the time of his arrival about a month ago. She had already been here. He recalled her as cool, distant, remote. Typically enough. Didn't want to know him or anybody else.

So the hell with her!

Little by little, however, over these past few weeks, she had—crumbled. Yes, right. Stopped washing her dress (and why did a girl like her seem to have only one?)—quit wearing tights (even though the weather was warm it certainly didn't explain the reason because she'd automatically put on what seemed to be her only pair long after they were holed at both knees)—quit shampooing her hair and altogether fallen to pieces. Often at night, during the past ten days, she had wept loudly enough for him to hear through the thin walls of the house.

Addict?

It would have been a logical answer. But he numbered a good few victims of the hard stuff among his acquaintances: cocaine, heroin, even opium.

And I'd take my oath she's not a junkie!

Which left precisely one possibility.

She's nuts!

Thankfully, he accepted that as the truth. Who'd want to tangle with a crazy girl? The Rowalls knew this here doctor, this Argyle. Let them and him cope.

His ear, bent close to the door, reported that Alfred and Bella had gone back into their own ground-floor section of the house. Cautiously he peered out. The coast was clear. Making sure that his room- and house-key were in his pocket, he hurried downstairs.

But as he was passing along the hallway, he caught a snatch of conversation which nearly stopped him in his tracks. He heard Bella say, in the living room:

"And don't you forget to phone Richard, find out if there's a quicker way to drive her crazy!"

Jesus God!

Clyde West ran.

"Ah, there you are!" boomed Dr. Tom Gospell as Nick entered the saloon bar of their favorite summer pub, the Horse's Neck. He was a burly man with a strong resemblance to a trained bear; today the likeness was enhanced because he was wearing a rough terrycloth shirt of nearly the same shade as the immense brown beard that cascaded down his chest. "Even if I wake you up in plenty of time, you still manage to be late! Well, I bought drinks for both of us at one sharp, and I've finished my pint and damn nearly finished yours as well—so it's your round!"

"Two more pints of draft bitter," Nick told the barman absently, leaning both elbows on the counter and staring in the general direction of a wall clock which confirmed that he was actually less than ten minutes behind schedule. But ever since they were at school together Tom Gospell had been poking fun at his friend's fondness for punctuality. Tom could arrive somewhere an hour late and carry that off with aplomb; Nick was the type who would begin to fret at the five-minute mark.

"Hey!" Tom checked his half-empty tankard on its way to his mouth. "Sorry, old son. What's the matter?"

"I—I don't really know. But . . ." Nick heaved a sigh. "Well, the weirdest thing just happened. I was on my way here, and I'd just passed Paddington Station, when a girl jumped into my car and started talking to me. In a foreign language, I think; anyhow I didn't recognize what she said. I spotted a needle-mark on her arm, and I thought oh hell, here's an acidhead coming down from a bad trip or—or something like that, so get lost. And . . . oh, thanks." He gave the barman the price of the beers which had just arrived.

"I hope she did," Tom grunted. "Acidheads and junkies I wouldn't wish on my worst enemy. I'm starting to think I was a fool to buy a practice in the area I did; I've had half a dozen persistent nuts around my neck for the whole of this week, and I just figured out why they went over the edge! What was she like, though?"

"Like? Oh, slim, fairly tall, blonde, quite pretty—no, cancel that: very pretty. And would you believe completely starkers under a dirty off-white coat?"

"Yes, I'd believe," Tom sighed. "What did you do with her—drop her off at the nearest cop-shop or outpatient department? I hope!"

"No, there was this woman waiting for a bus at a stop just ahead of where I pulled up," Nick said. "She turned out to know the girl—called her Sally—and promised to take her home. Her landlady, apparently."

"So why are you looking so worried? By what you've told me, you're well shut of the affair."

"It was the woman," Nick said, gazing now into his beer mug. "There was something about her, something sort of *nasty*. And I'm sure I've seen her before."

"Not surprising, if you live close by."

"No, not near where I live. Somewhere else—Damn it, that's it!" Nick straightened with such a jerk, he nearly spilled a drink being collected by someone behind him. Having apologized, he went on, "I do know where I've seen her before! Remember last summer, just after you graduated, you took a temporary job in Soho?"

"Oh, don't remind me!" Tom said, with an exaggerated wince. "You mean the time I stood in for Richard Argyle?"

"Yes! Wasn't there some kind of scandal connected with him?"

"Argyle came within the ace of being struck off the

medical register a few years ago, before they set up
centralized drug clinics," Tom said. "He was supposed
to be the doctor to go to if you wanted to get more
heroin and morphine than you were entitled to and sell
off the surplus. But over-prescribing for registered
addicts is a thing of the past. Mark you, as I think I
said at the time, having met a few of his patients I
was quite prepared to believe the worst of him. . . .
But what the hell does this have to do with the woman
at the bus stop?"

"It was in Soho that I saw her before. I was coming
to meet you at Argyle's office on Pulsifer Street. I was
on time but you were still tied up, so I hung around
for a bit. And she was on the opposite corner doing
the same thing, hanging around. Until a guy in a bowler
hat and pinstripe trousers came up and they started
chatting and then they went into one of the houses
nearby that she had a key for. Lord, it's coming back
as clear as yesterday!"

"Omigawd," Tom Gospell muttered. "Fancied her
yourself, did you?"

"You're joking! A blowsy dyed redhead with bags
under her eyes large enough for luggage?" Snorting,
Nick sank half a pint of his beer in long thirsty gulps.
"Did you order anything to eat? No? Then let's take
some sandwiches outside; it's too fine a day to stay in
this crowded bar. Barman!"

But he added, having placed their order: "To be
absolutely candid, Tom . . ."

"The one you fancy is the tall slim blonde," Tom
grunted. "Change your mind and make it fast. If she
isn't on drugs she must be out of her mind. Count
yourself lucky to have fobbed her off on somebody
else!"

Chief Inspector Dougherty's eyes were closed, and
his hands were folded on his ample paunch. After
lunch he was enjoying the warm afternoon in the
shade of his small garden's one and only tree.

He was just drifting into a contented snooze when his wife called from the open kitchen window.

"Bill, telephone! It's the Yard!"

"Say I'm not here," he answered, refusing to open his eyes. "Say I'm being held prisoner by the Mafia and I shan't be turned loose until Monday morning."

"But it's Sergeant Bray, and he says it's important!"

"Oh, hell. . . . OK, tell him to hang on."

Snorting, he rose and lumbered indoors. Picking up the phone, he said, "Yes, Bray, what is it? I warn you, your excuse had better be a good one."

"Sir, I wouldn't have bothered you at home if I hadn't been sure this was something you'd get angry at not being told about." Bray was long used to dealing with Dougherty. He concluded with a chuckle, which his superior echoed.

"OK, what is it?"

"It's on the taped report which Hedger brought in, sir. I'll play it over to you. I think it's pretty clear, but I have had a transcript made. Here we go."

Dougherty listened. Now and then he grunted. Eventually he said, "Yes, Sergeant. That is a very remarkable new development. But—ah—are we in a position to do anything about it?"

"I've already done several things, sir," Bray returned in a nettled voice.

"Such as?"

"Well, even though he didn't get the complete registration number of this red Jaguar, Hedger did get the letters, as you heard from the tape. We're tracing it now. He's certain it was an XK120, and there aren't many of those left on the road, so it should be quite easy to identify the owner."

"So when you find him, what will you do?"

"That's a good question, sir," Bray said apologetically. "At first I thought in terms of setting a watch at his house, but we're so understaffed. . . ."

"And into the bargain this is Saturday!" Dougherty barked. "Sergeant, I've been on duty an average of thirteen hours a day for the past six weeks and more than once I've hit sixteen hours! Suppose you leave me alone for a bit—please?"

"Yes, sir," Bray sighed, and cradled the phone.

V

That night an image haunted the dreams of Nick Jenkins: the face of a beautiful girl, drawn to thinness by near-starvation, with huge blue eyes eloquent of inexpressible suffering.

But when he woke and gathered his wits about him, he said to the air, "No, damn it! Tom's quite right— I'd be an idiot to get involved with a crazy girl!"

He had once seen it happen to a friend. It had been tragic.

It was as fine a day as yesterday. Weekend London basked in bright warm sunshine. This was weather for long-distance driving . . . except that the same idea must cerainly have occurred to a hundred thousand other people. When Nick turned on the radio news, he heard that there were monstrous traffic jams on all roads out of and near all big cities.

It had been bad yesterday when he brought Tom Gospell home from the promised excursion. He didn't fancy wasting any of today in a long stinking line of nose-to-tail cars.

On the other hand, he didn't fancy staying home, either.

Casting around in his mind as he shaved, he recalled that it was a long while since he dropped in for a Sunday lunchtime session at the Adelbert Arms.

That was a pub, within easy reach of his home, where an impromptu band got together every Sunday from noon until two P.M. A pianist who had turned up each week for years acted as informal leader, but it was never possible to predict whether today's band would have eight horns and three drummers, or three horns and eight people on everything from bongos to shac-shac.

Good idea.

Briskly he wiped the last smear of lather from his cheeks and hunted through his exiguous wardrobe for something that would be both smart and comfortable in this miniature heatwave.

On his arrival about ten past twelve, he discovered there had been changes since his last visit: the bars had been redecorated, and a totally different crowd of people thronged the premises. Still, the noise of the band was loud and cheerful. He pushed his way by a mixture of deceit and gall right to the bar, and was just waiting for a beer to be delivered when he caught sight of someone who looked familiar, a black man about his own age. The clients were black and white in about equal proportions, but there were many more white girls.

He said, "Hi there!" It was reflex. The guy looked at him with a blank expression, and in the same moment Nick realized what he'd done.

"I'm terribly sorry!" he exclaimed. "I thought we knew each other—but of course where I've seen you is on TV! Aren't you in an airline ad?"

The black man gave a wry grin. "Mm-hm. You in the same trade, are you? I mean, you're an actor?"

"Me? No!"

"Thought you might be. Just about every second person here seems to be a member of Equity, 'resting.' Same as I am."

Nick chuckled. "Then I'm one of the lucky ones. I just dropped by for the music. Have a drink."

"I don't know if I ought to. Last night I went to see a friend of mine and he gave me what was supposed to be rum and tasted more like metal polish and I drank too much of it anyway. . . . Hell, OK. Call it the hair of the dog. I'll have a vodka, though."

"Sensible."

After which, when there was a chance to talk against the music—it was loud today—they chatted desultorily until the legal two hours expired during which the pub could stay open at lunchtime on Sunday.

Emptying his last glass, Nick said, "Well, I'm on my way. Can I give you a lift?"

"Going anywhere near Paddington?"

"Why, yes. I live in Mulborough Square, just behind Sussex Gardens."

"The one with all the big houses carved up into apartments?"

"That's right."

"Lucky bastard. That's the sort of place I'd like to live in. I'm in a run-down alleyway called Mamble Row. Do you know it?"

"Ah, I imagine we can find it. Come on."

"Thanks very much, this'll be fine. Not that I especially want to go home, but I'm too broke to do anything else. Thanks again—see you."

"No, just a second, Clyde," Nick said, staring down the drab street flanked with narrow mean Victorian brick houses. They had exchanged names during their conversation. "You mean this is called Mamble Row? Hell, I drove past it fifty times and never knew its name."

"Man, you stay away from it!" Clyde said, with feeling. His "hair of the dog" had developed into several double shots, and he was weaving a little. "It's a place where bad things happen. I'd go look for another room if I thought I could find anything cheaper. . . . But I can't, and what's the good of dreaming?"

"What kind of bad things?"

"Shit, that's a big question! Oh—like the landlady is a tart, and sometimes she brings a client back for the night and I don't get much sleep because she specializes in people who want to be whipped until they scream!"

Clyde glanced along the side street. "Oh, yes: never a dull moment at Number 5! And on top of that . . ." He hesitated, biting his full lower lip.

"What?" Nick demanded.

Clyde shook his head. "Something I can't figure. There's this girl, in the room right next to me. They got a living room and a bedroom and a kitchen downstairs, see, and they rent out my room and the one next and the attic. And—oh, shit. I guess she's kind of touched in the head. But when I came out this morning, I saw they'd put a bolt on her door."

He shook his head in puzzlement. "Brand-new and shiny. A bolt on the outside. I don't get it."

"This girl," Nick said. "Is she a slim tall blonde with big blue eyes, called Sally?"

Clyde had been on the point of walking away. He checked.

"Hell, you know her!"

"No, I don't."

"Then what the—?"

"Never mind! But if anybody's touched in the head it has to be me. . . . Clyde, you think that girl's being mistreated?"

"I . . ." The black man hesitated, then gave a firm nod. "Yes, I do! I can't barely credit it, but yesterday I could have sworn I heard Bella—that's the landlady —say to her husband he got to call up Dr. Argyle— that's the doc they been getting in to see to the girl— and . . . no, it's too sick, I can't believe it!"

"And what?" Nick rasped, half out of the driver's seat with impatience.

"I wasn't drunk," Clyde said. "I wasn't stoned. I was sober as a judge whichever way. I swear to God I heard her say, 'Find out how quick she can be driven insane.' "

Nick whistled. Abruptly he glanced over his shoulder and put the car into reverse. He had drawn up the far side of the turning into Mamble Row; now he was able to swing into it and halt again next to where Clyde was standing.

"You do something!" he said.

"Like what?" Clyde snapped. "Ain't my business! I got problems of my own!"

"So have I, but this sounds worse. Just you pull back that bolt, OK? I'm going to stop opposite the house. I don't know how I know, but . . ." His hands were white-knuckled on his steering wheel, and a trace of sweat was running down his face. "But someone's got to help that girl!"

"Huh? But you said you don't know her!" Clyde countered.

"Is this doctor's full name Richard Argyle?"

"Yeah, right! I heard Mrs. Rowall call him Richard!"

"Well, if he's living up to his past form, the sooner that girl's out of there, the better. That man's reputation is pure poison!"

"OK," Clyde said with a sigh. "It's a deal. Just keep my name out of it if things turn sour."

In the time it took Clyde to reach the house, enter, go upstairs, Nick with furious rapidity had swung the car around in the narrow cul-de-sac of Mamble Row. Halting level with Number 5, he glanced up. There was a window on the first floor with curtains drawn. He sounded his horn loudly, once—twice—three times.

The curtains parted and a wan face framed with pale hair looked at him, disappeared. He sat there fuming.

And then, all of a sudden, just as he had concluded that his impulse was totally crazy—

A shriek, and a yell, and a volley of curses, and the house door opened and the girl came out at full pelt with nothing on but a sheet wrapped around her, and the instant he saw the door move he reached across to open the door of the car and . . .

Left shouting on the pavement: the dyed redhead he had seen not only yesterday, but last year too in Soho. Left shouting on the front steps of the house—its entrance floor was above street-level, because it had a basement fronting a below-ground "area"—a man going bald, with a weak chin, his expression dumbfounded.

Here in the car: the same blonde girl as yesterday
But this time she wasn't uttering some kind of non
sense word. She was saying, "Quick! Get us away from
here immediately! I don't know why you're doing this
but I was never so grateful in my life!"

Nick stamped on the accelerator and swung around
the corner with a squeal of tires, heading homeward.

Two blocks distant he had to slow the car for a red
light. His hands were slippery with sweat and he was
losing his grip on the wheel. He said, "To be honest, I
don't know why I'm doing this, either. But—well, is it
true you're being treated by Dr. Richard Argyle?"

"How the hell did you know that?" She stared at
him.

"You have a Jamaican friend of yours to thank for
mentioning it."

"What? Clyde West? But I hardly know him!"

"Never mind, he was the one who told me. Are you
being treated by Argyle or not?"

"Treated?" She gave a harsh laugh, and drew the
bedsheet which was her only covering more closely
around her; a couple of pedestrians were staring at her
in fascination. "He hasn't been *treating* me! Bella
Rowall called him in—that's the woman who dragged
me out of your car yesterday—but he won't listen
to anything I say, just gives me all these injections
that are supposed to help me sleep and don't stop me
having terrible nightmares. I don't want injections, I
want help! I must be crazy and I don't want to be
crazy and I don't want to be driven crazy!"

That echo of what Clyde West had said made
Nick's spine crawl as he wrove on. He said after a
pause, "Sally, tell me something about yourself. Who
are you?"

"I don't know. I wish I did. I've lost my memory. It's
as though a thick curtain has been drawn across most
of my mind, and no matter how I struggle I can't see
through it."

He glanced at her in pure astonishment. "Lost your

memory?" he echoed. "But that doesn't necessarily mean you're crazy."

She set her chin at a mutinous angle.

"I'm sure you're right. But what if you get back a memory that isn't yours?"

VI

Baffled, Nick drove the rest of the way in silence. It was not until he turned into the handsome square where he lived that he uttered another word.

Then, on seeing the white-rendered porches of the houses, their gaily-painted windows and frontages, some with striped summer awnings, the neat island of grass in the middle with benches under shady plane trees, Sally exclaimed with delight, and came near to clapping her hands with joy, forgetful of the need to hold her sheet together.

Parking the car and switching off, he said with a sigh, "Sally, my reputation around here is bad enough already. Please don't make it worse. Come on, indoors quickly!"

"What are we going to do, what are we going to do?" Alfred Rowall moaned as he returned to his living room.

Slamming the door behind her, his wife snapped, "Oh, stop it, for God's sake! We'll do what has to be done! Did you get the number of the car?"

"I . . . no, of course not!"

"Then you can bloody well be thankful that I have more wits than you do!" Bella strode over to a side table, found a pen and scrap of paper, wrote rapidly. "Right, get on the blower, find your chum Terry if it takes all afternoon and all night as well. He can trace car registrations, can't he?"

"Well, only—"

"Yes, only the kind that collectors might pay a lot of money for! Well, you take a look at that number! It'll be a bloody miracle if he doesn't have it on his list! Go on, hurry!"

"What are you going to do?"

"Find out how the girl escaped, what else?" Bella stamped her foot in sheer exasperation. "Christ, if she broke the bolt off the door . . . ! I told you you've never been fit to stick on a postage stamp!"

"Ah, shut up," Alfred grunted, heading for the phone.

"I will not! I have more right to talk than you do. What kind of a mess would you have landed us in if I hadn't been here? And that's no thanks to you—it was just that the Test Match finished early so I was able to collect the full weekend's takings yesterday."

"So you bloody told me. Look, if you're going up—go! And don't make too much of a row or you might get that nosy black fellow interfering."

"Is he back?" Bella said in astonishment.

"What do you mean, is he back? Of course he's back —came in just before the girl ran off. . . . Oh."

Alfred's voice trailed away.

"I never heard him! Just before the girl got away . . . are you sure?" Bella took half a step toward him.

"Damn right I'm sure!" Alfred said between his teeth. "And if he was the one who— Come on, let's sort him out!"

"It's like a dream, like a dream!" Sally whispered as Nick ushered her through the front door of the house and hurried her up one flight of stairs toward his own apartment, located on a sort of half-landing. And she said it again as she entered his rooms. More strictly: *room*. Once it had been enormous, twenty-five feet long with an eleven-foot ceiling and a fine view over a private garden behind; it would perhaps have been the original owner's master bedroom. Even subdivided into a bachelor flat, with a tiny kitchen and an even smaller bathroom slotted into what had been the dressing area, it was still like heaven after Number 5 Mamble Row.

And there were things everywhere: shelves of books, more shelves of records, a stereo hi-fi, a color TV, a dining table with four chairs, an armchair, a convertible bed, a . . .

It was no use. Sally shook her head, dazed, as she tried to comprehend what it was like to own so many *things*.

"Here!" Nick said. She roused from her moment of confusion to find that he was offering her a bright green terrycloth bathrobe. Promptly she seized it and contrived to wrap it around her without losing hold of the bedsheet until she chose to. The roughness of the material was like a lover's caress, because for the first time in what felt like an eternity she was surrounded by cloth that was absolutely clean.

By gentlemanly reflex Nick had glanced toward the window while she was donning the robe. Now he stared at her with his full attention.

"OK, here you are," he said. "Now the question is, what the hell do I do with you? I suppose the sane first step would be to contact the police, find out whether anybody's hunting for you. How long ago did you lose your memory?"

Sally look embarrassed. "I don't know."

"Oh, come on, girl! Weeks—months?"

"I suppose . . ." She bit her lip. "Probably several weeks. It isn't actually that I can't remember. I mean, after I got there, to the Rowalls' place, my memory kept on working fine. But each day has been so much like the next, the next, the next . . . they've all blurred together. I haven't seen any newspapers or watched TV or anything. I knew it was Saturday yesterday because that's the day the old woman on the top floor carries out her kitchen rubbish. I recognized that. But I don't know if I've heard it five times before, or six, or seven. . . ." She gave a helpless shrug.

"Have you contacted the police yourself?"

"No, and I don't know why!" Sally exclaimed, slam-

ming fist into palm and striding toward the window.
"Oh, God, aren't you lucky to live in a nice place like
this . . . ? I—"

She checked. "I just realized! I don't know your
name!"

"Oh—Nick Jenkins."

"I'm Sally Ercott." She turned back from the window
and sat down on the arm of the nearest chair. "Eternal-
ly indebted to you! I can't hope to explain what life
has been like for me these past weeks, because I don't
understand it myself. I mean, we haven't really come
very far in your car from Mamble Row, have we?"

"About three-quarters of a mile," Nick grunted. "If
that."

"And yet I'm farther from the Rowalls' house than
I've been since I arrived there." Sally shook her head
dismally. "It was as though something was tugging me
back every time I tried to leave! The last time I managed to go out on the street was—oh—must be ten days
ago." She rubbed her left wrist. "I pawned my watch
because I'd run out of money. I was behind with the
rent. . . . But—but *hell!*" The robe had fallen apart to
show her knee; she slapped it furiously. "I didn't want
to rent a room, there or anywhere!"

Nick said slowly, his eyes on her face alert for any
sign of dishonesty or deception, "What's the earliest
thing you can recall? When did you—uh—come to, as
it were?"

"I remember walking up Mamble Row. It's not a
through street for cars, but there's a passage for pedes-
trains at the far end, a shortcut. When I got to Number 5 I looked up and saw a sign advertising rooms to
let. I don't know why I went in, but I did!" She clenched
her fists. "And there I was in that horrible dirty room
saying yes, I'll take it, here's a month's rent in advance.
I had a purse with me, and there was quite a lot of
money in it. But I don't know what became of it afterward."

She licked her chapped lips.

"And then . . . maybe I passed out, I don't know.

Anyway, I found myself, a bit later, there in that disgusting room, and I didn't know why I was there, I couldn't recall where I'd been going or anything about my past life—nothing at all! Nothing about relatives, friends. . . . *Nothing!*" Her voice peaked to a shrill note of despair. "And it's been that way ever since, only worse!"

"Relatives," Nick said, snapping his fingers. "Did you look your own name up in the phone book?"

Her jaw dropped unashamedly. "No! There were phone directories in the Rowalls' living room—I saw them—but it never occurred to me. . . . Nick, do you see what I mean when I say I'm crazy? I must be, surely, or I'd have had that much sense!"

"Ah, if you think you're crazy the chances are good that you aren't, just scared of getting that way." Nick reached at full stretch toward the phone table; it was a little wheeled trolley with the directories underneath. He selected volume *S to Z*. She checked him with a gesture.

"No, what you want is *E to K*. Lots of people make that mistake and think my name is Urquhart, U-R-Q. Actually it's Ercott, E-R-C. . . ." Her eyes lighted up suddenly. "My God!"

"What's wrong?"

"Nothing's *wrong!*" She jumped to her feet. "But . . . oh, Nick, you must be a miracle-worker! I'm sure I haven't had to explain that to anybody since I lost my memory, yet it sprang right into my mind. That's the first time I recalled anything from my past!"

With the fat book on his knee, he gazed earnestly at her. "Literally?" he murmured.

"Very nearly, I swear. I mean, apart from basics— my name is Sally Ercott, I'm twenty-five years old. . . . But that was where it stopped." Disconsolate, she corrected herself. "I mean stop*s.*"

"I see." He flipped the pages of the directory, then set it aside. "Well, add another consolation to your short list. If you had looked up your own name you wouldn't have found it. Must be quite rare."

"All that leaves is the police, then—isn't it?"

"I suppose so." He replaced the directory and hooked his fingers under the phone trolley to draw it toward him. Abruptly, however, he canceled the gesture.

"You know something? I think there might be one possibility before that. I'd like to avoid it, for your sake."

"Why?" She blinked at him; then her face fell. "Oh, no! You don't mean you think I may have done—done something terrible, that the police would be after me for?"

He looked at her levelly. "Well, you said you were getting back a memory that isn't yours. I'm no expert on this sort of thing, but I believe one of the commonest causes of amnesia is that your subconscious is refusing to accept some really loathsome recollection. Assault, for example. So it might be a good idea to try to sort that out before contacting the police, hm?"

He leaned forward. "And there's something else . . . this Dr. Argyle!"

"What about him?"

"He has an unsavory reputation, to say the least."

"Oh, *that* wouldn't surprise me! Christ, he'd been bad before, but yesterday when the Rowalls routed him out on a Saturday afternoon . . . !" She shuddered.

"Yes, what did happen after you jumped in my car?"

"Oh!" She groped in the air as though searching for untraceable words. "I let Bella take me back . . . but it wasn't as though Bella were in charge of me. Something seemed to be tugging me along that was for more powerful than her. I mean I detest her; if I never see her again that'll be too soon. They dumped me in my room, and she and her horrible husband held me down and took away my coat. I'd left my panties in the bathroom, and they took those, and the rest of my clothes were on a chair, and they took those. It was revolting!" She closed her eyes and her mouth twisted as though she had bitten into rotten meat. "They kept me there—didn't even let me go to the bathroom and

I had to use the only thing there was, a wastebasket! Luckily it had a plastic lining. . . . And then Dr. Argyle turned up in a filthy temper, and by then I was hysterical, I suppose, so he wouldn't listen to me, just gave me *another* jab and this time handed over a syringe and some vials of some sort to Bella. . . . Ugh, Nick! *Ugh!*" She looked as though the wanted to vomit. "It's been pure hell! When I looked out of the window and saw your car, I just didn't believe it. And then when I found I could open my door—I'd tried it, and it was bolted from outside—I threw that sheet around me and I ran like hell, so terrified that even if I did get to the street you wouldn't be there any longer. But at least the effects of the last shot must have worn off. I feel pretty much OK now, except that I'm very weak."

"You look it," Nick said. "When did you last have a square meal?"

"Oh." A wan smile. "Maybe a week ago. I've been surviving on what I could cadge: sandwiches, the odd glass of milk. . . ."

"Right." Nick rose decisively. "I never keep much food in store, but I think a bowl of soup, and a boiled egg or something . . . not too much until your tummy gets used to the idea of food again."

"Oh, marvelous! But—uh—could I please have a bath first?"

"A bath?"

"I feel so filthy, as though dirt had soaked right down to my bones!" She pointed at her tousled greasy hair. "I can't bear the touch of my own skin, and when I think that strangers have seen me in this ghastly condition I want to puke!"

"Go right ahead," Nick said. "I'll have the soup ready when you've finished."

VII

The moment the bathroom door closed behind Sally, Nick snatched up the phone and dialed a number he knew by heart. Mentally he crossed his fingers as the ringing tone went on and on . . . but eventually he heard the familiar voice of Tom Gospell.

"This is Nick," he said in a soft urgent tone. "Listen, Tom, the most amazing thing has happened and I need your help."

"Hmm! Must be your week for amazing things. What is it this time—a whole harem?"

"Shut up and listen! This is serious! The girl I told you about yesterday—she's here at home with me now, and I want you to come and take a look at her."

There was a pause. Eventually Tom said dully, "Oh, Nick, I wish to God you'd taken my advice. I told you: don't get mixed up with a girl who's mentally unstable! And how the hell did you track her down, anyway?"

"I'll tell you in a moment. But the point is, I don't think she is crazy. She's just amnesiac, or so she says."

"Then let her go to hospital, or find her own bloody doctor!"

"That's just it. Her landlady—the woman who hauled her out of my car like I told you—she sent for, of all people, Dr. Argyle. And he's been jabbing her full of something which is supposed to be a sedative and obviously isn't."

Tom whistled; the shrillness of the sound in the phone made Nick wince. "I'll be damned! Your trick memory must have been working overtime again. I remember you said you'd seen this woman near Argyle's office."

"Right. And given the bastard's reputation . . ."

"Yes, agreed. But . . . oh, damn. Do you absolutely insist on my calling around? Why don't you turn her over to the nearest out-patient department?"

"Because I think what's been done to her is a hell of a sight more serious than it looks. You see, I went to the Adelbert Arms, and . . ." He summarized his encounter with Clyde West.

"Drive her out of her mind?" Tom said foggily when he'd finished. "And you took that seriously? The unsupported word of someone you ran across in a pub? That's why you rode to the rescue like a knight on a red charger?" He uttered a snort of disgust.

"Tom, for pity's sake, *will* you come and take a look at her?"

"Ah, hell . . . yes, OK. I have a date with Gemma again this evening, but she doesn't come off duty until six, so I can spare a couple of hours. But all I can say is that you are a ruddy nuisance. I was looking forward to my first free weekend for a month, and here you come up with an extra patient for me. . . ." A resounding sigh. "OK! I'll be there in about half an hour. No, make that forty minutes. I've been basking on the balcony and I'll have to shower to get rid of my suntan lotion. See you—*idiot!*"

Oh, this is absolutely ludicrous!

One minute after doing as Nick Jenkins had asked, and silently drawing back the bolt on Sally's door and realizing that that wasn't enough and giving it a good loud bang, Clyde West wanted to kick himself. Having vanished into his own room, he heard three blasts on a car horn outside. A pause; Sally's door opened. Through a crack he watched her rush downstairs with a sheet as her only garment, and out of sight in the hallway he heard the Rowalls cry out. Shutting his door, he hurried to the window just in time to see Sally jump into the red Jaguar and roar away.

Almost at once the screaming match between the Rowalls started up, and it struck him forcibly that—whatever their reasons for keeping Sally captive—now she'd got away it wouldn't take much intelligence to figure out who had released the bolt. . . .

Christ!

In place of a wardrobe, this room had a hanging rail in one corner, with an old velvet curtain around and a hardboard lid above it. Feeling like a complete fool, Clyde darted toward it and hid inside the curtain.

And found he wasn't being foolish. Shortly there were footsteps on the stairs, and a knock on his door. He stayed put. He heard Alfred say, "But I'm sure he did come in! Got the key to this room?"

"Here," Bella said, and thrust it in the lock. Clyde shivered.

Then:

"Well, he isn't bloody here, is he?"

"Maybe he went out again," Alfred muttered. "Who else could have unbolted the girl's door, hm? Must have sneaked past while you were screaming at me!"

"Oh, shut up! Come on, you get hold of your pal Terry—we've got to trace the owner of that car!"

The door shut again.

Clyde had been holding his breath. He let it go with a gusty sigh. What in the world were these people up to? He recognized the name Terry; they were referring to Terry Jones, a crony of theirs, who apart from his regular trade as a rented-car driver had a lucrative sideline, buying and selling cars with distinctive registration numbers so that the original vehicle could be scrapped and the number transferred to some wealthy braggart. His greatest achievement, which he never tired of describing, had been to secure FEB 29 for a hotel proprietor born on that date.

And . . . hmm! That Jag of Nick Jenkins' had a pretty distinctive number. Clyde couldn't recall exactly what, but he had noticed that there were three identical letters and three identical figures.

So Terry might well have it on his list of items to be traced, might already have found out who the present owner was with a view to bidding for it. In that case life was about to become tough for Nick Jenkins.

Still, let him do his own worrying. It had already become tough for Clyde West. Stealing cautiously out of his hiding place for fear the floor might creak and give away his presence, he sat down to ponder his next course of action.

Exactly what consequences had flowed from what Chief Inspector Dougherty had termed his "smart work" of yesterday, Detective-Constable Stan Hedger didn't know. But they must have been important. Here he was with the chief heading westward across London on a Sunday afternoon in what looked like a regular taxi. It wasn't. It was standard transportation for officers of the Covert Crime Squad, because nobody ever looks more closely at a cab than is needed to see whether the on-duty sign is alight, but it had been intensively modified. Since its introduction, this model had often astonished car thieves or villains making their getaway from a robbery by displaying better acceleration and road-holding than the average ˙ports car.

He said diffidently, "Sir, I'd like to ask a question."

"Such as?" Doughtery grunted, producing and filling a charred old pipe.

"Well, I don't mean to pry, and anyhow it was made clear to me when I joined the Covert Squad that there'd be times when I had to do things without knowing the reason, because one leak and a whole operation might go to waste. But I do think it would help if I knew a bit more about this one."

Dougherty applied a match to his pipe. He said through a cloud of blue-gray smoke, "Yes, I think you're entitled. Go ahead and ask."

"If Bella Rowall is turning over the sort of money you'd expect, why do she and her husband live in that horrible narrow street overdue for demolition? Surely they could afford a pretty plush apartment, or even a house, in a good district."

"But Bella isn't at the top of her class," Dougherty answered. "She about middling. But better known than the general run of Soho professionals, because of that flaming head of dyed hair, but nothing more. She has to pay through the nose for the room where she entertains her clients, and what's left over—her take-home pay, as it were—is just about right for a small terraced house. We dug into that and it's been confirmed."

"OK, if she's run-of-the-mill, why does she rate such a large-scale operation? When Argyle arrived on the scene, I thought ah-hah, here comes the star of the piece. But according to what I've been able to find out, his days of—ah—glory are over for good and all."

"Right," Dougherty said with a nod. "Not to mention his days of illicit tax-free income. Now he's running a sleazy practice mostly patronized by whores and strippers. Oh, I imagine he takes the odd lump sum under the counter when a nightclub manager doesn't want us to hear about the guy who got carved up by the local frighteners last night, but that's petty cash stuff. No, setting up the centralized drug clinics ended the one business Argyle was really good at, peddling under the auspices of the Health Service. We keep tabs on him, naturally, but . . ." A wave of his arm sowed a line of pipe smoke across the interior of the cab.

"So two second-raters and an inefficient pimp are involved," Hedger said, frowning. "Doesn't figure. Is the really important person the girl?"

"We don't know," Dougherty said. "But it's unlikely."

"Oh, hell!" Hedger exclaimed, and caught himself. "Excuse me, sir. But honestly I'm getting so frustrated—! Don't I deserve the rest of the facts?"

"As a matter of fact, I'd already arranged clearance to give them to you," Dougherty said with a chuckle. "It goes like this. You know Missing Persons has been snowed under for the past few months?"

"Yes, of course."

"Some very irreplaceable people have gone spare, from all over the country, for absolutely no apparent motive. Several wealthy businessmen—a Scottish golf professional—two moderately well-known pop singers. . . . All sorts. It took one hell of a long time to find any link between them, and we had to sift through some of the most private parts of their lives." The chief inspector gave a sudden harsh laugh. "Private parts! Damn right! Never thought of that before, but it's literal. Turned out, to cut a long one short, they did have something in common, a particular kink."

"Serviced by Bella?" Hedger demanded, leaning forward.

"Very likely. We managed to get wives and girlfriends and psychiatrists to open up about things you ordinarily can't reach. Maybe this permissiveness bit does have advantages. . . . Anyhow: the kink they shared was the idea of being dominated by a red-haired woman. Along, of course, with all the trimmings: boot-licking, whips, being tied up. . . ."

Hedger shuddered. "Never could understand people like that!"

"Try harder," Dougherty said. "You won't be a detective until you do. . . . As I was going to say, though: funnily enough that wasn't the route we got here by. Along with all the people whose disappearance made headlines, there have been dozens—scores—of perfectly ordinary blokes. For instance, football fans up in London for a cup-final match, who boasted to their mates later on that they'd celebrated their team's win by a roll in the hay with a red-headed tart. And so on. All of which still might not have pointed us in the direction of Bella Rowall, but that over the past eight months twelve people who have vanished completely turned out to have lodged at Number 5 Mamble Row."

Hedger whistled. "You mean she and her old man have been making away with people?"

"No, and that's what's driven us to mount this size of operation. We've watched both Bella's place in Soho and her home for six mortal weeks, and as yet we haven't seen one customer go in who didn't come out, one lodger who left any other way except the way you might expect, in a small moving van complete with luggage. They don't disappear directly from Bella's clutches. They vanish anything up to a fortnight later." He clenched his fists. "It's a bastard, this one! It's a *brute!*"

 VIII

Oh, bliss! Oh, paradise!

Though the bathroom was tiny, so narrow she could span it with her arms, the tub was full-sized and the water was deliciously hot. Sally sank luxuriously into it. Nick had told her to help herself from a jar of pine-scented salts kept on a tiled shelf; she had tossed in three extravagant handfuls and the perfume was wonderful.

Moreover he had set a bottle of shampoo ready on the end of the tub, and in a few minutes she would reach for it. For the time being, however, all she wanted to do was soak away the aches and miseries of the resent past.

Echoes survived, against her will: *I wonder what my home was like. I'm sure I had one, sure I was comfortable and happy there. . . .*

But now that she was away from Mamble Row, the cloud of terror which had haunted her had disappeared. She felt a sense of confidence. She had finally found someone who talked to her sympathetically. She would be given a rational explanation for her weird hallucinations. She would be helped and ultimately cured.

What a miracle that the total stranger I picked on was a man willing to bother about me! So many people, after the way I acted yesterday, would have run a mile on spotting that I was around!

That was somehow eerie. So too was the next thought which crossed her mind:

52

Funny! He hasn't asked about my reason for jumping into his car. Just as well, maybe, since I couldn't possibly give a rational answer. Even so, it's rather odd. . . .

To distract herself, she roused and opened the shampoo, then arched backward to dunk her head and wet her hair the lazy way.

Instantly—

Laughing among the other girls in the shallow pools left between the rocks by the retreating tide, she wrung water from her hair, then shook her head so that a spray of drops flashed like jewels. In this heat it would dry soon enough. She climbed out of the pool in which she had been rubbing herself and stretched happily. The air and the water were alike crystal-clear; the sky was a brilliant, wonderful blue, and the red rocks and the reddish-brown sand rolled down to the deep green sea.

Two of the other girls had brought a ball; seeing her rise from her bath, they invited her to join in their game. Not bothering to wrap around her the single length of cloth which served as the garb for men and women both in this pleasant climate, she delightedly agreed.

Soon all the girls had finished their toilet. Some opted for the ball game; others preferred to lie down in the sunlight and doze or chat about their boyfriends. Much time had passed enjoyably when a girl who had happened to glance seaward uttered a cry of fright.

Concealed until a moment ago by a rocky headland, four ominous black shapes loomed into view. They were ships—large ships. They cast anchor where the water was as deep as a man's waist, and soldiers poured from them and came splashing toward the shore. It could be seen that they were tall and strangely clad. Each brandished a double-bitted ax or a mace.

She had the ball in her hand; she was standing on a rock in the center of a ring of her companions, tossing it to each in turn. Now, horrified by the sight of the *strangers, she dropped the ball and took a reflex step backward.*

Losing her footing, she fell, into a pool exceptionally deep. The sucking sensation of water closing over her face mingled with pain as her head struck something hard. There followed darkness.

Choking, she realized there was actually water in her mouth. Flailing her arms, splashing, spluttering, she managed to sit up, and for a long moment had to cling to the side of the tub. She was trembling.

"Sally?" From beyond the door, Nick's voice. "Is anything the matter?"

"N-no," she forced out. "I'll be out in a few minutes. I'm just going to wash my hair."

"Are you sure you're OK? It sounded as though—"

"I put my head too far under," she snapped. Which was as near the truth as made no difference.

"Oh, I see." A faint chuckle. "Well, don't do it again!"

It was more than a few minutes, though, before she had regained enough control of herself to continue bathing. That unexpected vision had been so real!

Like the rest. Every single one had been so incredibly vivid . . . !

Quite simply, they didn't feel like dreams, or delusions. They felt precisely like genuine memories.

It's as though all recollection of my former life has been bodily scoured from my brain, and these non-sensical bits and pieces substituted.

Somewhere there ought to be knowledge of childhood, parents, school; of friends, perhaps lovers, conceivably a family of her own. (That idea was purely terrifying. But she was certain there had been no ring on her finger when she arrived at the Rowalls', so it was most improbable she was married.)

How can I explain this to Nick? I must explain what's happening, must must, and let him believe it or not!

"Soup's hot!" he called, and at the words, for the

first time in days she experienced a pang of honest hunger instead of a dull sour empty feeling which made the mere idea of food revolting.

"On my way!"

Scrambling out of the bath, she wiped herself hastily with the towel Nick had set ready, then knotted it around her still-wet hair and donned his big rough robe again.

When she emerged, he was just ladling out soup into an earthenware bowl. Glancing up, he said, "I don't have to ask if you're feeling better. I can see you are. Want some bread to go with your soup?"

"Yes please!" She sat down at the table. "All of a sudden I'm ravenous."

"Take it slowly," he warned. "You don't want indigestion on top of all your other troubles. . . . By the way, I made a phone call while you were in the bath. Somebody's going to call around and look you over."

With the first spoonful of soup poised before her mouth, she checked and stared at him. "Who?"

"One of my oldest friends, a guy I was at school with, is a doctor with a practice near here. Name of Tom Gospell. Matter of fact, after he graduated he had to make ends meet by acting as a *locum tenens* for six months, and among the people he deputized for was a certain—ah—Dr. Argyle."

She almost dropped the spoon, and a look of haunted horror flared in her face.

"Whom he learned to loathe in next to no time!" Nick added sharply. "Sorry, I didn't mean to shock you like that. I was going to explain that it's purely because he has met Argyle that Tom's willing to do me the favor of stopping by here on a Sunday." He bit his lip. "I wish I'd been able to tell him more about you, though. Is there absolutely nothing you recall bar your name and age?"

"My size in shoes," she said helplessly. "The fact that I like ravioli. Irrelevant scraps. Don't think I haven't tried to remember more. I've lain awake night after night wrestling with myself, but it's like trying to walk through a wall." She hesitated. "But every now and again I've had—well—snatches . . . which don't make sense."

"You said," Nick prompted, "something about getting back a memory that isn't yours."

She nodded.

"Was it by any chance a—a *snatch* of that sort which made you cry out in the bath?"

"Yes," she said with an effort.

"When you've finished your soup, tell me about it."

So, after pushing aside her empty bowl, she drew a deep breath and complied. Nick's face remained totally impassive until the end of her story; then he suddenly uttered a gasp.

"Foof! I was completely on the wrong track. When you said 'a memory that isn't mine' I thought . . . well, something abominable, like I said before: maybe rape? I never expected to be told about savages with battle-axes charging up a bright red beach! Oh, Sally, that's *weird!"*

Emboldened because he hadn't chosen a far stronger term, she said, "Not half as weird as the one I was still involved in when I jumped in your car."

"I was wondering how soon you'd tell me why you did that. OK, lay it on me."

She did so. This time he looked positively startled.

"Ay-ay-ay! If you don't mind my saying so, I'm glad I'm not inside *your* head. A creature under a mountain stealing away human beings to sow its young—horrible!"

"I tell you something very strange," Sally said after a pause. "It didn't seem nearly as horrible as you might imagine, because it was something I'd—well, grown up with. Or to be more exact: not me, but the person I was being. She was revolted and frightened, yes; but she was far more angry than either."

Before Nick could comment, the doorbell shrilled. He jumped up.

"That's probably Tom. I'll let him in. Won't be a moment."

As well as his medical bag, Tom arrived bearing a large paper sack full of beer bottles, which he thrust into Nick's arms immediately the door opened.

"Here! I'm not going to have the whole of my Sunday ruined, and I know you never keep any rations in the house. . . . The girl still here?"

"Yes, of course."

"And . . . ?"

Moving slowly toward the stairs, Nick said in a thoughtful voice, "When I phoned you I was in two minds about her story, you know."

"As who wouldn't be? Now she's convinced you, I presume."

"No, that's the damnable thing. I'm certain she's in desperate trouble, I'm certain she wants help and is pathetically glad that she's found somebody she can talk to. On the other hand, she just told me the most incredible yarn. Hang on a second and listen to this."

Rapidly, he recited the content of the two visions Sally had told him about, shorn of all but their most essential details.

Tom gaped unashamedly. "She refers to those as *memories?*"

"I'm quoting. What I've been wondering . . ." Nick hesitated; they had halted on the landing outside his door, and he kept his voice low for fear of Sally overhearing.

"Yes?"

"Could this somehow be due to what Argyle's been pumping into her?"

Tom plucked at his beard. "Offhand, I'd say no. The hallucinogenics have never been a specialty of mine, but since it turned out that a few of my patients are going down the primrose path I have read a couple of supposedly authoritative books, and I never saw mention of any dope that could entrain such a coherent system of fantasies. . . . Hell, what are we doing standing out here? I'll ask the girl herself!"

IX

At Tom's entrance Sally rose diffidently and said, "You must be Dr. Gospell. It's terribly kind of you to—"

"None of that, young woman," Tom boomed, dumping his medical bag on the table. His irascibility had dissolved, to be replaced by bluff joviality. "Nick told me you were pretty enough to bother with on a Sunday, and he's quite right. Well, I'd better start by laying violent hands on you, I suppose. I gather you've lost your memory?"

"That's right."

"OK, let me take a look at your head. Eyes first, I think." He opened his bag and produced a miniature flashlight, which he switched on and off to check the battery. "Had any trouble with your eyesight? Eyestrain? Double vision? Headaches?"

"Nothing like that. I mean, apart from what's due to worry and sleeping badly."

"Nightmares?" Tom prompted, rolling up first one, then the other of her upper lids and flashing the light into her pupils.

"Yes, dreadful nightmares."

"In spite of being given sedatives?"

"If what Dr. Argyle gave me was a sedative, it must be the worst in the world!"

"I see." Tom held up a finger in front of her face. "Focus on my fingertip while I move it back and forth. . . . Fine. Open your mouth, please. . . . Fine.

Pulse, please." He held her wrist for a few seconds, let it fall.

"Pupillary contraction normal, accommodation normal, throat clean as a whistle, pulse on the high side but you're obviously agitated so that's no surprise. Now let me have a feel of your scalp."

Undoing the towel around her head, Sally said apologetically, "I'm afraid my hair's still wet."

"It's beautiful hair but I'm only interested in what's underneath." His large blunt fingers probed every square inch of her scalp with improbable delicacy. Eventually he gave a satisfied grunt.

"No trace of any blow, though of course it might have healed by now. . . . How long since the trouble started?"

"I've been explaining that to Nick. The nearest I can estimate is about six weeks: not less than five, not more than seven. Sorry to be so vague, but where I was lodging every day was identical with every other except for weekends. Things got muddled."

"A fair time, anyhow. How is it you haven't been taken to a hospital to have your skull X-rayed? I'd have thought that was the first thing Dr. Argyle would have done."

She shrugged, her expression resigned. "Well, he didn't. As a matter of fact, he didn't even carry out the tests you just did."

Tom whistled. "If that's true, the man's an even worse GP than rumor says. I'm not supposed to slander my colleagues, but I don't regard Argyle as a colleague and no one is going to force me to! Right, Nick had better turn his back or shut his eyes. I want to examine the rest of you. Keep your undies on; that'll be OK."

"I—uh—I haven't any. The Rowalls stole my clothes and I had to run out of the house wrapped in a sheet."

"Quite true," Nick put in. "And I've been wondering what I can do about that. I think I got the answer." He headed across the room toward a chest of drawers at the far side of his convertible bed. Over his shoulder he added, "Tell me when I can turn around again."

"Will do. Young lady, peel off anyhow. I have to check your reflexes and posture and one or two other things." Tom bent to his bag again and laid in a row on the table a stethoscope, a rubber hammer, and a portable sphygmomanometer.

Flushing a little, Sally discarded the bathrobe. For a few minutes there was no sound in the room bar an occasional muttered order from Tom: "Cough please. . . . Again. . . . Breathe deeply. . . . Sit down and cross your legs. . . . Stand up, shut your eyes, stand as still as you can. . . ."

Then at last he said, "OK, put your robe back on. That's the lot."

Nick closed the drawers he had been rummaging through and returned to them carrying a new pair of stretch summer briefs, not out of their cellophane pack, a clean but faded pair of bluejeans, and a cotton T-shirt.

"I imagine these will fit, more or less," he said. "You may have to roll up the jeans, but they're three years old and they date back to when I wasn't just slim but skinny, so with luck they won't be big enough to fall down. On the other hand the T-shirt may be a trifle tight. . . . Still, it's the best I can offer, I'm afraid, unless you'd rather wear one of my regular shirts as a minidress. And I have no idea what to do about shoes; all mine would be far too big."

"Not to worry!" Sally said, eagerly accepting the clothes. "I often go barefoot in summer, even on pavement. . . . Hey!" Her face shone. "This is fantastic! That's the second time since I got here that I remembered something about my—my past!"

Nick glanced at Tom, who had restored his gear to the medical bag and snapped it shut.

"Even little snippets could be useful," the doctor said. "Carry on."

Smiling, she darted into the bathroom to get dressed.

The moment the door swung to, Nick said in a low tone, "Find anything?"

"Needle-marks. A dozen of 'em. Argyle's doing, presumably. Apart from that, and not having had enough to eat for much longer than a week, she's in excellent health. Next question: if the cause of her amnesia isn't physical, what is it due to?"

"Could it be physical in another sense? I mean chemical?"

"Blazes, I told you just now: I never heard of any kind of dope that gives rise to the effect you described! Weren't you listening?" Tom sighed heavily. "But you've persuaded me about one thing."

"What?"

"This girl isn't insane in any conventional sense. I'd better have a chat with her, hear her story from the horse's mouth. You get some glasses for the beer, hm? It may take a while."

Nick nodded and made for the kitchenette. As he slid open the door of the cupboard where he kept his glasses and cups, Sally reappeared, and Tom gave her a broad grin.

"Very nice! Very nice indeed!"

It was true; with her hair sleek from washing close around her shapely head, she looked lovely. And if the T-shirt was in fact a fraction tight as Nick had predicted, that wasn't any sort of drawback.

"I—I feel nice," she said. "The real change is inside. It's due to having someone take me seriously."

"Sit down," Tom said, pointing to the nearer of Nick's two armchairs. "You're going to be interrogated, young woman. Nick, where's that beer, damn it? And pour a glass for Sally, too. It's my informed medical opinion that it won't do her any harm and may even help her to unwind a bit." He dropped into the other armchair himself, gazing at her thoughtfully.

"First of all, I want you to go over what you were telling Nick before I got here."

"You mean about my—my visions?" Sally said, accepting her beer from Nick.

"That's not the word you used before," Tom murmured.

"No. But they do *feel* like memories! I suppose they must be—oh—hallucinations, delusions, whatever. Only they *feel like memories!*"

Tom swigged a long draft of his beer. Setting down the glass, he said in a musing tone, "Ever experience what they call *déjà-vu*, the 'I've been here before' feeling?"

"No. At least I don't think so. And"—with an appealing glance at Nick—"it's the sort of general thing I might remember, isn't it? Like knowing I'm used to not wearing shoes in summer."

"That sounds like a fair point," Nick conceded. "Tom?"

The doctor's only response was a grunt. "I'm listening," he added atfer a moment, and Sally launched into a repetition of her recital.

"Is that the way she told it before?" Tom said when she finished. Nick nodded.

"A few changes of emphasis, a couple of extra details. Otherwise yes."

Sally stared at them both hungrily. "Dr. Gospell, what do you think?"

"Tom's my name. . . . Frankly, Sally, I don't know." He emptied his glass for the latest of several times, and hauled himself to his feet. "I never ran across any case like yours before."

"Can't you even tell me if I really am insane? I mean, I feel I must be—it simply isn't normal to have visions like mine!—and yet . . . I don't feel weird, peculiar, disturbed. Not right this minute, anyway. Back at Mamble Row, yes; since I arrived here, I've been feeling so much better. I'm not manic, I'm not depressed, I'm not talking some private jargon of my own, I'm just getting these incredibly clear mental impressions." She shook her head; her hair was nearly dry, and fluffing out to its original condition.

"I think that's a valid point," Tom said, frowning. He hesitated, then glanced at his watch. "Look, I tell

you what. I have a date with my girlfriend this evening
—she's a nurse and she comes off duty at six—and I
don't want to be late. But if I leave you now and go
straight home, I can look at a couple of books and
see if I can contact a person who may have some useful data. I can't phone from here because his number's
unlisted, but I have a note of it at home. Nick, if I
find out anything I'll let you know later. OK? So long,
Sally. Look after Nick, won't you? He's an old friend,
you know."

"You've been wonderfully kind," Sally said. "I'm
sorry to impose on you both."

"Ah, Nick can't complain. He landed himself with
you. . . . Right, I'm on my way."

"I'll see you out," Nick said. "Won't be a moment,
Sally."

"Of course. . . . By the way! Can I borrow a brush
and comb? I'd like to untangle my hair."

"In the bathroom, middle shelf. Help yourself."

On the stairs Nick said, "Do I have to tell you that
this whole scene fascinates me?"

"Given your fondness for tall slim blondes and your
peculiar warped mind, it does add up. What are you
going to do with her now?"

"Oh . . . I just remembered a place near here that's
open on Sunday where I can get her something to put
on her feet—beach sandals, that kind of thing. And I
suppose I'll have to take her for a bite to eat later on."

"What about dropping by at the police station to ask
if there's a missing-person file on her?"

"I know I ought to do that, but . . ." Nick bit his
lip. "Well, what's holding me back is the fact that
Argyle is involved."

"I see. You're afraid she may have done things that
could land her in a mess."

"More or less."

"You mean you're going to keep her here? Indefinite-
ly?"

"Of course not! But I can't afford to put her into

a hotel, you know, and just in case she is off her rocker I don't want to wish her on any of my friends including you, so . . ." A shrug. "I've camped on the floor often enough when somebody missed the last train home."

"Listen, old son," Tom said solemnly, "make that the floor and no two ways about it, understood? Even if she's willing, even if she's eager, even if she's bloody pleading, don't get that mixed up with her until you're satisfied she doesn't have any screws loose. None whatever! I like you too much, you know, to want to see you hung up over a nut-case."

Nick gave a sour grin.

"Yes, grandpa! But don't worry. I know perfectly well that's good advice. Talk to you later, then. So long."

X

"MP to Covert Kilo," said the scrambled radio on the dash of the disguised taxi. The driver took the mike and acknowledged.

"We have those car registrations for Chief Inspector Dougherty. The Jag XK is registered in the name of Nicholas Kenneth Jenkins and you're right outside the front door of his last notified address. The white Mini is registered in the name of Thomas Walter O'Brien Gospell. He's a doctor with a practice in North Kensington."

"Anything known about either of them?" Dougherty demanded.

"No, sir. No convictions, no file, no nothing."

"Thank you. Covert Kilo out."

Returning the mike to the driver, he sank back in his seat and uttered an enormous sigh.

"This damned case gets worse and worse! About the only consolation is that this Jenkins character seems to have done the sensible thing and put the girl together with a proper doctor. Apart from that . . ."

He tensed, staring across the road. "Someone's coming out."

But it was the owner of the white Mini, whom they'd seen arriving an hour ago: a burly man with a big tawny beard, carrying a black bag.

"Mike again, please," he muttered. The driver passed it. "Covert Kilo to MP and scramble, please. . . . Bray!"

"Yes, sir!"

"Anything from the Mamble Row watchpost since last time I inquired?"

"Not a thing. No sign of either of the Rowalls, or of West. Mrs. Ramsay went out as usual on Sunday to visit her sister. That's it since the girl ran off."

"And the girl hasn't left Jenkins' place and so far as we know there isn't a back exit. Right! This is the one ex-lodger of the Rowalls' whom we are not going to lose track of. Find me a couple of men to start a permanent watch at this location."

"But, sir!" Bray's voice was full of dismay. "We're terribly shorthanded as it is, and it's Sunday and—damn it, sir! I wouldn't know where to start looking!"

"I don't care how you do it," Dougherty grunted. "Just do it. Covert Kilo out."

Glancing at Hedger, in the back seat next to him, he added, "Are you sure you want to be a detective for a living? It doesn't look nearly as romantic close up as it does on television, does it?"

Hedger gave a wry smile.

"No, sir. But I tell you what: from here it looks a hell of a sight more like real life."

Dougherty chuckled, and after that they went on waiting.

Sally tugged and tugged at the knots in her hair, her mind only half on the task of unsnarling them.

What had that doctor really thought about her story?

No doubt, when Nick went to the door to see him out, he'd wanted a confidential last word about her. Well, fair enough. It was miraculous that she'd found people willing to listen anyway. And certainly they were both very nice. . . .

She laid down the comb and took up the brush instead. Perhaps it was vain of her, but she tried to concentrate on her image in the mirror, because the sight of herself so transformed after the dirt and grime of recent weeks was itself a tonic. No, more still: a psychological link with the past actuality she had imagined gone forever.

And then, without warning—snap!

The splendor of her clothes was dazzling. Around her hips was a skirt of thinly beaten gold leaf, appliquéd on a heavy silky fabric. Over her shoulders and crossing on her bosom were two magnificent panels of brocade, embroidered with fertility symbols and luck charms in red. Her slender waist was girdled with a belt of red and yellow hide; on her head was a crown of feathers and shells that towered almost her own height above her, so heavy that her neck ached. Green paint outlined her eyes; red, her lips; blue, the fine veins on the backs of her hands. There was a ring with a stone set in it on each finger and every stone differed from its neighbor. Round each of her great toes was a tiny leather strap with a bell attached, jingling as she moved. A necklace of solid metal plates an inch square clung at her throat. Even the sour-tasting elixir they had given her to drink could not prevent her reveling in the fact that she was adorned with the most gorgeous bridal array in a hundred years.

"Sally! *Sally!*"

A shout. She roused with a start, and found Nick staring back at her from the mirror. He was peering through the doorway, his expression concerned.

"Sally, are you OK?"

"Oh, I'm fine!"

"But you were just standing there, absolutely rigid—like a statue," Nick muttered. "I thought you must be having another of your attacks."

She hesitated; then she passed the brush one final time through her newly-resplendent tresses and turned to face him.

"Yes, I was."

"In that case how can you say you're all right?"

Chuckling, she walked past him into the living room. "Because this time I didn't mind. In fact I quite enjoyed it. Yesterday it would have shaken me to the core. I'd have burst out crying from sheer terror. But now I feel so much calmer, so much happier. . . . And it's all thanks to you and your friend. Nick, I could kiss you, I really could!" She turned a glowing face to him.

But he didn't respond. Instead he waved her to the chair she had used before and sat down where Tom had been.

"What was your—your vision this time?" he demanded.

"Oh, I saw myself as a bride. Looking what they call radiant, I suppose." She laughed. "You really are working miracles for me! That's the first which hasn't been unendurable."

He hesitated, studying her. At length he said, "I'm afraid even if that T-shirt is white it doesn't look much like a bridal gown, you know."

"White?"

Suddenly, seeming giddy, she put her hands to her head.

"White?" she said again. "But I wasn't wearing white. I was dressed up in all kinds of colors, red and yellow and gold, but no white." She tensed. "*I* wasn't white! I saw my face, and I was more—more copper-colored!"

She swallowed hard. "I felt wonderful, I felt this was the greatest day of my life, but . . . You know something? If you hadn't mentioned it, I don't honestly think I'd have realized it wasn't *my* face I was admiring in the mirror. I saw myself as the person I'd been since I was born, and that was that. Nick, in heaven's name what can be happening to me?"

He evaded a direct answer. Rising, he said, "I've remembered where I can buy you something to put on your feet. Only flip-flops, I'm afraid, but if you tell me your size I can go and get some for you. What you ought to do, I think, is lie down and rest while I'm gone."

"It's awfully kind of you," she muttered. "And if I'm going to the police, which I'm sure I should, it wouldn't make much of an impression if I arrived barefoot, would it? But I'd rather not be left on my own. I can't explain why. I just have a feeling that something might . . ." She interrupted herself.

"You're beginning to wonder what you've let yourself in for, aren't you? I don't blame you. I'd feel the same way. There simply isn't anything I can do, though. No money, no friends, no—nothing."

"I know precisely what I've let myself in for," Nick said. "I'm helping out of a lot of trouble one of the prettiest girls I ever set eyes on. She may have so much trouble that she needs more help than I'm equipped to give. In which case somebody else will have to take over. For the time being, though, let's carry on."

With a shy grin, engagingly boyish, he beckoned her toward the door.

As they descended the stairs, she said, "Nick, tell me something about yourself. All I know is that you're a nice kind helpful person. But—well, what do you do?"

For no apparent reason, he flushed as he held the street door open for her. "As a matter of fact," he said, "I'm an inventor."

"What?"

"It's perfectly true." There was a hint of sharpness in his voice, as though to disguise embarrassment. "Most people think of inventors as absentminded old men who spend their time in garden sheds that are liable to blow up without warning. But even if I'm not a terribly successful one, that's what I am: an inventor."

"What have you invented?"

"Oh, that's a long story. But . . . well, you see, when I went to college I wanted to study something practical. I like working with my hands as well as my head. So I signed up for an engineering course. The professor of my department was also a part-time consultant to a big corporation, and now and then he used to discuss industrial problems with the students, to show them the sort of thing they'd be involved with when they graduated. And . . . it's hard to explain, but Tom says I have a warped mind, which I suppose is a fair description.

Anyhow, I came up with the solutions to a couple of their worst difficulties, and the professor was duly impressed. Having an ambition to lead an easy life when I left the university, I went to the corporation and said look, these ideas which are making you so much money are due to me—if you don't believe it ask my prof—and there are thousands more where they came from, how about hiring me as a consultant too? I don't know where I found the necessary gall to convince them, but they put me on an annual retainer. I'm not sure it was such a great scheme after all, though," he added with a scowl.

"But it sounds marvelous!" Sally exclaimed. "What went wrong?"

"Basically, I let them sign me to a five-year exclusive contract. What looked like a lot of money compared to my student grant, thanks to inflation, has become a pittance. Still, I oughtn't to complain. The five years will be up next summer, and I'm sitting on a stack of half-baked notions which are of no interest to them but should be to sundry other firms. . . . There you have it."

She said musingly, "Nick, don't you think it's amazing that out of all the millions of people in London I should have picked on someone like you with—well, an open mind?"

"Yes." He gave her a sidelong glance. "That's one of the things I plan to talk about over dinner. You said you like ravioli; I presume that extends to Italian food in general?"

"Nick, you mustn't! You've done far too much for me already!"

"Think of it this way. Suppose we'd met at a party. If I asked you to have dinner with me, would you say yes?"

"I think so." A smile quirked up the corners of her mouth.

"OK, we met at a party. Cross the road here; the place we're making for is around the next corner on the left."

XI

The store was a self-service minimarket open on Sunday chiefly for emergency groceries, but it had a display of cheap Hong Kong slippers and sandals. Sally pronounced herself perfectly satisfied with a simple pair of flip-flops.

Leaving the store, she clutched at Nick's arm.

"Oh, you're being so kind, so generous! I'd stopped believing in that sort of thing. The world has been so full of monstrous menace."

"So you told me," Nick said dryly. He glanced at his watch. "Hmm, I see we have time on our hands. The pubs don't open until seven on Sunday around here, and . . . are you ready for dinner yet?"

"Goodness, no. I'm still full of soup. Give me at least another hour."

"Right, then. Let's go sit on a park bench and chat. I know a pleasant little square near here, like the one where I live but nicer, with lots of flowers."

"Oh, feeling free like this is wonderful!" She almost danced as she followed him along the street.

A few minutes later, they sat down side by side under a handsome plane tree facing a bed of colorful antir-rhinums and geraniums. No one else was nearby except a middle-aged couple trying to persuade a poodle that it wasn't really constipated.

Suddenly she turned to him.

"Nick, when you went downstairs with Tom, you

must have wanted to talk about me without my over-hearing, right?"

"Ah . . . yes."

"Did you come up with any ideas?"

After a brief hesitation he took her by the right hand and silently pointed a long thin finger at the many needle-marks on her arm.

"You think my trouble might be due to something Argyle gave me?"

"It struck me as what they call a tenable hypothesis." She shook her head. "Absolutely not."

"Why?"

Because, for one thing, I started to get these visions long before the Rowalls sent for him. In fact it was because I was sick and faint after having one of my—uh—attacks that they first called him in."

"I see. About how long was that after your arrival?"

"Oh, goodness! That was quite recently. I must have managed to get through at least a full four weeks before I let anybody else find out what a hell of a mess I was in. I think it was realizing that my rent was overdue and I had no more money which tipped me over the edge."

He pondered that a moment, then said, "So that must have been around ten days ago?"

"Maybe twelve, near as I can figure it out."

"OK. You said 'for one thing'—is there another?"

Sally frowned. "I don't know for sure, but I suspect so. I suppose really I should have raised the point when I was talking to Tom. . . . What I get isn't a simple flash, like looking at a photograph. It's a whole awareness."

"I'm not sure I follow that," Nick muttered. He felt in the pocket of the loose light jacket he was wearing and drew out a packet of cigarettes. "Smoke?"

"No thanks, I don't—" Startled, she stared at him. "Now that makes the third time today I've remembered something about my previous life. . . . No, it's not significant, is it? I had a purse when I arrived at the Rowalls' and if I were a smoker I'd have had cigarettes or matches or a lighter, and I didn't. I had the impression you didn't smoke either, though."

"Never before six in the evening, and we're past my deadline." Lighting up, Nick glanced around the little patch of grass and flowers. A young man in a blue blazer, open-necked shirt, and silk scarf, had come to sit on another bench and leaf through a Sunday newspaper. He seemed to be paying them no attention.

"I presume what you mean," Nick went on at length, "is that your visions aren't just detailed in themselves, but extend beyond what's actually happening in them. Is that about right?"

"Yes, exactly!" Sally said in excitement.

"OK, give me some examples. What about the one which drove you out of the house and into my car?"

"Oh, yes! It was full of—of associations, and overtones, and implications . . . I don't know how to put it."

"Try. Start this way: you said you *talked* to the creature under the hill. How come it spoke Eng—No, how come it spoke a human language?"

There was silence between them for a moment, during which she gazed at him, eyes wide. She said at length, "Nick, I think you must have started to believe me. You're quite right. I understood what it said, which wasn't surprising because I—no, *not* I but the person I remember being at the time, *she*—knew it was intelligent and could compel humans to come when it called. But the language it spoke in certainly wasn't English. I can still hear an echo of the actual sounds." Dazed, she put her hands to her temples. "But I can't even begin to imitate them! My throat and tongue don't work that way!"

Nick waited. Eventually she continued, "It's logical, I suppose. I mean, there never has been such a creature, so . . . but this is the hell of it. I remember so clearly not just that meeting with it, but all that went before: the shape of the hill, the countryside around, the city where I lived—everything!"

"So describe the city," Nick invited.

"It was quite big, and it had wide roads, but the buildings were only one story high. There were carts and handtrucks, but no cars or even horses. Oh, yes: the streets were paved with rough stone and there were deep ruts because the stones were so old. In the middle there was one very large building and that was a temple which nobody visited anymore. When people first came to the place, they used to offer sacrifices to try to stop the creature in the caves from stealing away more of the young men and girls, until they realized that that was the only sacrifice it was interested in and they gave up. They became sort of resigned to losing a few of their friends every year, the way we've become resigned to a few people we know being killed in car crashes. I—uh—I seem to be talking nonsense, but you asked for it."

"Not at all. As a matter of fact it's starting to hang together."

"Really?" Her face lighted up with hope. "Oh, explain!"

"Not so fast. Tell me more. Ah . . . yes, when you were telling me how you played with other girls on a red beach, you mentioned not a city but a village. What was that like?"

"Oh, a settlement of a few hundred people. No road or streets, just cobbled paths. People grew vegetables and went fishing. There was a lot of fish in the sea. Young girls like me didn't have to work until we were betrothed, when we were taught to cook and weave and keep house, and—and something else I was very much afraid of." Sally had to swallow. "I'd only heard about it, I didn't know any of the details, but the words that come to my mind now that I'm thinking it out are silly ones, like—well—magic, and witchcraft. To do with keeping the community safe, anyway."

"Go on!"

"I'll try. Yes. We were supposed to play on one side of the island and the boys on the other. They had to start much sooner learning to make nets and harpoons and catch fish, because sometimes there weren't enough of them left to—to do all the jobs that had to be done. Only of course sometimes we managed to creep across the island, especially at night, and meet our boyfriends in the woods at the top of the hill. But we never got really involved with them. It was too often the case that we made a date and the boy just wasn't there anymore."

"This hill: it had a monster under it?"

"I—uh . . ." Sally licked her lips, staring into nowhere. "It certainly wasn't the same hill, but perhaps. . . . No, I don't remember any more."

She leaned toward him beseechingly.

"If it's starting to make sense for you, then please *please* tell me how! It's happening to me, and I can't make head or tail of it. I'm desperate to hear your suggestions."

"My best suggestion," Nick said, grinding his cigarette underfoot, "is that we adjourn to a pub I know. It's opening time and the air's getting cool."

"But—!"

"Please don't argue." Taking her hand, he rose. "It's true I have an idea, but it's far too new for me to want to talk about it. Come on."

Depressed, she followed him.

The pub he led her to, sited on a corner, was modern and smart and newly-decorated. Cheerful music was playing. As he held the door for her to go inside, two barmen in crisp white jackets glanced up expectantly.

"Right," Nick muttered. "Straight across and out the other door."

"What?" She almost stopped dead in her tracks.

"Don't argue, do as I say—I have my reasons and I promise you they're good ones. Hurry!"

Confused, starting to wonder whether some fearful mischance had involved her with someone even crazier than she imagined herself to be, Sally stumbled out the far door.

"Nick, what the hell is all this about?" she demanded.

"Round the next corner to the left, twenty yards or so along, and I'll tell you—but for heaven's sake, girl, get a bloody move on!"

There was another pub around the corner: shabbier, older, occupied at present by three elderly men in shiny suits staring at a small color TV set; there was sports news. Nick ushered Sally to a vacant bench in a corner where they had a clear view of the bar door. Unlike the former, this pub opened only on one street.

"Sorry about that," Nick murmured. "But—ah—well, did you happen to notice that a young man in a dark blue blazer was taking a great and unjustified interest in the window display of the store where we bought you those sandals?"

Sally's jaw dropped.

"Not the same one who was sitting on the park bench near us?"

"Yes indeed. So I wondered whether he might decide to go for a drink at the same time as us, and bingo, he folded his paper and trotted after within about thirty seconds. Which is why I went through this rigmarole. Sorry. I can think of lots of reasons why he might be following you—after all, he looked at a loose end and you're more than pretty enough to catch any man's eye. What I can't figure out is why he's following *us*."

"Nor can I," Sally whispered. "Unless . . ."

"Yes," Nick said. "Unless. And there are all kinds of nasty ideas running through my head. You look pale. Something to steady the nerves might be in order. How about a brandy?"

XII

"Damnation," Dougherty muttered, staring out of the back window of the cab. "I hoped that might be whoever Bray found to set up a watch here. But it's Hedger coming back and he looks miserable. . . . Give MP another buzz, will you? Find out what the hell is going on."

The driver nodded and reached for the microphone.

"You lost them?" Dougherty demanded as Hedger climbed in.

"Afraid so, sir." Hedger wiped his face with the display handkerchief from his blazer. "It's true I haven't had much practice at tailing people, but I swear I don't know what I did to tip him off. Still, it wasn't coincidence that enabled him to lose me. It was deliberate, and what's more it was downright professional."

"How did it happen?"

"Oh, he marched the girl into a pub with two entrances—called the Duke of Sutherland—and straight out the far side before I felt it was safe to follow. I spun the usual sort of yarn to the barmen, about being sure he was an old friend, but they didn't know him and when I got out on the other street myself, no sign of either of 'em. . . . Sorry, sir."

"Probably not your fault," Dougherty sighed. "Lord knows what the girl can have told him, but obviously it's made an impression. He likely thought you were a hatchetman working for the Rowalls. . . . Driver, I thought I told you to raise MP again!"

"Yes, sir," the driver said in an injured tone. "Sergeant Bray is ready and waiting."

"Then sling me the bloody mike!" And seizing it, Dougherty went on: "Any progress?"

"Chief, I've hunted high and low and I literally can't find one spare man for an additional watchkeeping job. Not even to take over at Mamble Row in place of Hedger, when Prior comes off duty. I've done my best, and there isn't anybody at all."

"Ah, shit," Dougherty said with feeling. "Well, if we can't we can't and there's an end of it. Mamble Row is a sight more important than this place, anyway. Right, just do the usual: get authority to put a tap on Jenkins' phone, see if we can collect any clues that way, and issue an all-cars watch for his red Jag. No action, just a report of its movements."

"Yes, sir. Anything else?"

"When I think of it. Covert Kilo out." Dougherty returned the mike and added, "Back to the Yard, driver."

"Why the hell should Jenkins have shaken me off?" Hedger demanded in an aggrieved tone, more to himself than to his superior. "Come to that, why hasn't he run the girl around to the nearest police station to lay a complaint about the Rowalls?"

"I don't know," Dougherty said. "And at the rate we're progressing, I honestly think I never shall."

When brandy and ginger ale had put color back in her cheeks, Sally said, "Do you think the man who was following us could have been sent by the Rowalls?"

"How should I know?" Nick sighed. "At least if we hadn't shaken him off he'd have joined us by now, so we can forget about him for the time being. Go on telling me about these visions of yours. I have this ridiculous feeling that there's a pattern to them. Lord knows what, but . . ." He shrugged and took a gulp from the glass of beer he had bought himself. "Well, it's my talent, inasmuch as I have one. I make patterns out of odds and ends that other people overlooked."

Sally hesitated. At last she sighed. "Yes, OK. But the more I review what I—I *seem* to remember, the more absurd it appears."

Nick gave a sudden chuckle. "Personally I never let that interfere. I didn't tell you, but one of the inventions I came up with at the university was a gimmick that couldn't work. My professor said so, the reference books said so, the experts at the company said so. . . . Being a pigheaded bastard I went ahead and did it anyway. It was a matter of constraining the gyroscopic precession of a centrifuge to fine down the rate at which— Excuse me. I talk too much about myself and anyhow I'd get dreadfully technical if I went on. Point is, I have this habit of taking seriously things that other people dismiss out of hand. It wastes a lot of my time, and theirs, but now and then it pays an unexpected dividend."

"It's paid off for me," Sally said, and impulsively clasped his hand.

"You may be convinced of that, but I'm not. Not yet. Go on talking. Or—Wait a second!" Nick snapped his fingers. "Can you draw?"

She pondered, frowning. "Yes, I think I can. Why?"

Nick fished in his pockets and produced a draftsman's pen, another with a fiber tip, and a small plain notepad.

"I like putting things on paper," he said. "You've described your—uh—experiences in words. Let's find out whether your visualizations are clear enough to turn into pictures."

"I'll try," she said dubiously, accepting the pens and pad. Tongue between her teeth like a school child, she stared a while at the blank white surface, then suddenly started to make strong firm strokes with the fine-point pen, broad smears of shading with the fiber-tip.

"There!" she said in triumph. "That's one of the men who came up the beach from the four black ships."

Nick studied her sketch thoughtfully. He said at length, "Does anything strike you as—well—odd about him?"

"Well, no—not unless you mean: do I keep running

into armored barbarians wielding battle-axes?" was Sally's tart response.

"And this is a reasonable likeness?"

"Yes! Matter of fact, it's better than I expected."

"And it doesn't seem strange that you've given him four arms?"

For the space of a dozen heartbeats she sat absolutely rigid. Then her face crumpled as though she were about to weep.

"I didn't notice," she muttered. "But how could I not have noticed? There's only one explanation. I have to be out of my mind. Nick, surely your friend Tom must refer people to mental hospitals occasionally? Couldn't I be sent somewhere and treated properly?"

"You," Nick said, "are talking trash. Stop it."

"What?"

He drained and set aside his glass. When he next looked at her she seemed to be meeting a different person. Until now there had been a kind of diffidence in his manner, frequent hesitation in his speech, frequent unfocusing of his eyes as though he were looking through instead of at her, his mind not fixed on what she was saying but on some unformulated hypothesis.

That was gone. His gaze was level and his voice incisive.

"You said you were lucky to hit on me out of all the people in London. Suppose you cancel luck from your calculations; what are you left with?"

Puzzled, she shook her head.

"Come on, come on!" he rapped. "I don't believe in luck! I do believe in chance—have to, it's the basis of modern science. *Well?*"

"It was millions to one against my hitting on you, I know that!" she said with a flare of annoyance. "But what does that prove?"

"Absolutely nothing. But it does signify." He leaned earnestly toward her. "Look, I'm fairly sure you aren't crazy—excuse that 'fairly' but one is supposed to maintain a detached attitude. Who else had you tried to talk to about your problem since it overtook you, inside or outside the house where you were lodging?"

"Nobody at all, until today," she confessed.

"Including the doctor who quotes on and off 'treated' you. So we have this situation: the *very first time* you explain your trouble to somebody, it turns out you've found a person with—uh—a warped imagination." A faint grin. "It reminds me of what they say about intelligent life."

"What's that?"

"We've explored exactly one planet. Intelligent life has evolved on it. Logically, the incidence of intelligent life is one hundred percent."

"Damn, I thought you were being serious."

"Oh, I am . . . in a way. A unique phenomenon must be taken at face value until you find evidence to the contrary. So scrap luck, scrap simple random chance. What's left?"

"I can't think of anything. Except . . ."

"Except what?" Nick prompted, leaning earnestly forward.

"Uh . . . somebody—something—planned it that way?"

"Near, but not exact. More: *it was necessary.*"

She thought about that for a couple of minutes. Eventually she gave a hesitant nod.

"Good! Now that should be enough to chew on for a bit—and speaking of chewing on, I'm hungry. Must be the heavy brainwork. Let's adjourn to a nice quiet restaurant."

Hungry? Yes, I am. Can be again. Fantastic. But . . .
In the act of rising to her feet: snap!

People grew very hungry in that bad season. Game was scarce and ice lay thick on the river. The winter closed its jaws on the village like a trap.

Old, toothless—useless—she huddled shivering in a corner of the hut with nothing to cover her but one old stiff animal hide, its fur worn bald. When she tried to approach the fire the young ones crowded her away. Many of the garments they wore layered one upon another against the bitter air had once belonged to her, and had been stolen regardless of how she might rant and rave and threaten to haunt them when she died.

For days now there had been no meat in the pot, not even a carcass found frozen to death in the snow. At first the babies had cried ceaselessly, but now they were too weak to utter a sound.

Yesterday already her grandson, new head of the family, had started to cast resentful glances at her. Now he spoke of what was in his mind, saying that the old woman was far past child-breeding, had become no more than a gaping mouth depriving everybody else of precious food. His wife, the woman from the next valley who had always hated having to defer to an older female, chimed in with the suggestion that there must even so be meat on her scrawny frame. . . .

Her grandson nodded, picked up his hunting knife and advanced menacingly toward her.

Sweat was streaming down her skin and there was the taste of terror metallic in her mouth. Yet the whole vision could have lasted at most—what?—ten seconds, and Nick seemed not to have noticed. He was at the door, poised to open it and let her out of the bar ahead of him.

In which case . . .

She gathered the maximum of her self-control. Nick had offered her what she most desperately wanted: a link with that near-imaginary, that *imagined* yet familiar past to which she desired with all her being to return, that world of security and comfort and occasional luxury which she had lost on arriving at the Rowalls. Lost? *Mislaid* might be a better word. So much of what had happened to her today awoke echoes of a vanished reality.

And these visions of mine can't possibly be real!

Clinging for all she was worth to that crucial concept, she hurried to catch up with Nick.

XIII

I must have been crazy to get myself mixed up in this. . . ! Now here I am reduced to hiding, damn it, in a room I pay good money for!

Slumped in the shabby armchair which apart from the bed offered the only place to sit, Clyde West stared moodily at the wallpaper and wondered when he might get the chance to sneak out of the house. The Rowalls were still downstairs, and he could imagine that they were on watch for him.

What have I got mixed up in? I can't make any sense of it at all!

Suddenly he brightened. He could hear the Rowalls emerging from their living room, making for the front door. By now it was growing dusk; he judged it safe to creep to the window, which was ajar at the bottom for the heat, and peer out. He not only saw, but distinctly though faintly heard, the Rowalls as they went out.

"I wish that bloody nignog would come back," Bella said viciously. "He won't know himself in the mirror when I'm through with him."

"Yes, he must be in cahoots with this bastard Jenkins," Alfred agreed. "Ah, there's Terry. Come on!"

A car which Clyde recognized, the car belonging to Terry Jones, had just turned into the short dead-end street. The Rowalls rushed toward it, jumped in, and issued urgent orders. Terry swung around and headed back the way he had come.

Waiting, Clyde reviewed what courses of action were open to him. All seemed to be out of the question bar one. He would have to leave the house while he had the chance, get a friend to put him up for the night, hunt tomorrow for somewhere else to live, come back for his belongings only when he could rope in a couple of muscular acquaintances by way of body-guards. . . .

Ah, shit!

But at least the coast was finally clear. He darted to the door.

The latest miracle to overtake Sally was that they were in a small friendly restaurant full of the scent of delicious food, with check cloths on rough wooden tables and candles in iron sockets on the walls and an attentive waiter handing each of them a menu.

She said, "This is so fantastic I can't believe it! In a way it's even harder to credit than my visions, be-cause . . . well, because it's what I feel life used to be like, the old life that I've forgotten."

"Not surprised," Nick grunted. "Campari soda, yes? Two, please"—to the waiter, who departed. He went on, "When we get you sorted out, it'll turn out you have a boyfriend all set to go by the ring. Wouldn't blame him. Wants to settle you down in some nice country town and raise a lot of children. You're not a London-er, are you?"

"No, I'm from—" Almost, the answer sprang to her lips. But it died. She slapped her menu shut.

"You set me up for that!"

"Any objections? If so, why? Don't you want to find out where you hail from? Or is all this stuff about visions just a way of masking the fact that you hated the place and everybody in it?"

He glared at her; it was like staring into white-hot steel. Yes indeed, here was a very different version of Nick Jenkins.

Almost inaudibly she said, "Do it again. Do it again, as often as you can. It hurts like hell, as though something's being wrenched loose inside my head. But I'm sure it's right. It feels—like you said—necessary."

"Sorry," he said in a milder tone. "But it might help, you know, if you were a bit more candid. You had another attack just before we left the pub, didn't you? But you haven't told me anything about it."

"You did notice!"

"What made you think I didn't? Don't worry; I'm sure no one else paid attention. But . . . well, you see, so long as you don't open up at once, there's bound to be a vague suspicion at the back of my mind that you aren't telling me the truth. See what I mean? I could say to myself, 'Yes, she is getting some kind of attack, but afterward she tidies up what she remembers to make a more impressive story. . . .' Like embroidering an illogical dream. Are you with me?"

She nodded dully. "I should have thought of that. It's—oh, reflex, I suppose. Habit born of not having had anybody to talk to, not even wanting to run over these crazy pictures in my own mind again. Still, that seems to have changed. I mean, the visions aren't half as horrible as they were at first . . . nasty, but not paralyzingly awful."

"What did you see this time?"

She described it as best she could. The waiter delivered their drinks; she left hers untouched until she finished, then drank half of it at a gulp.

"I see," Nick said with detachement. "And this— this grandson who attacked you: what was he like?"

"He didn't have four arms!" Sally snapped. "But if you want me to draw him, I'm sure I can."

"Go ahead."

Again she took his pens and paper and in a few rapid strokes executed the would-be cannibal's likeness.

"There!"

Nick studied it so long she had to ask shrilly, "What's wrong this time?"

"You honestly can't see it?" He handed back the drawing. She gazed at it in near-desperation.

"No, it's absolutely right!"

"OK, OK. But in that case, why is his head as round as a cannonball? You haven't given him any hair or ears."

Swaying, Sally touched her own blonde tresses. "I—I couldn't," she forced out. "He had ears like a snake. Just a slit through his skull, and an eardrum hidden inside."

She swigged her drink and concluded with defiance, "So did I!"

"Curiouser and curiouser," Nick murmured. "Decided what you want to eat yet?"

"Nick, how can you be so—?"

"Six impossible things, but *after* dinner. What about gnocchi, veal olives with risotto and salad, and Valpolicella?"

"I . . . yes, marvelous! Nick, does anybody ever pin you down to one subject for more than two minutes at a time?"

"Generally speaking, no." He relayed the order to the hovering waiter, and reclaimed the notepad to look over her drawing again. "You know, what puzzles me about these visions of yours is their extraordinary consistency. Like plodding through a swamp."

"What?"

"Apologies. Another fault of mine, a taste for abominable puns. It must all be linked with my allegedly warped personality. Tends to annoy people, pretty often."

Surprising herself, she said, "I like it. I like you. I think I might very well remember if I'd ever liked anybody more than I like you, and I don't."

"Well!" He blinked several times. "That's a hell of a nice compliment, and I don't know what to do with it. Mind if I postpone consideration of it for a bit? I was just about to ask for further details of this latest vision. Did it come—ah—wrapped, like the others?"

She nodded.

"OK. Now you said you were starving and freezing and the rest of it. How come your—your tribe hadn't made any proper preparations for winter?"

She put her hand to her mouth in dismay. "Nick, I'm beginning to believe you can read my thoughts. Of course, *that* was why I'd quarreled with my grandson and his wife."

The waiter deposited their gnocchi on the table; she ignored her portion.

"You see, I was old enough to remember the end of last winter, and I'd been told by—oh!—my own grandfather, or somebody, what it had been like. I knew you had to take special precautions, and that idiot wouldn't pay attention. Right back to when I was a little girl I could remember quite clearly. I can picture everything in my head here and now: ice flaking off the eaves of the huts, the floe jams breaking in the river, every day the suns rising higher in the sky—no, I must mean the sun. . . . No, that's not right."

She gave him a hurt look. "I did say 'suns,' didn't I? Not 'sun'?"

He nodded.

"Well, that's what I damn well meant. Suns plural. Two of them. Very small and side by side."

"That fits. A planet in orbit around a double star would have to swing out incredibly far in order to be stable. No wonder your winters could outlast a person's lifetime."

During the pause that followed they simply looked at one another while their food grew cold on the plate. Only when the waiter arrived with their wine did Nick find the energy to stir.

"Oh dear," he said. "Oh dear, oh dear! I don't know if I just made the greatest intellectual breakthrough in history, or whether what Tom is pleased to call my skeptical credulity finally caught up with me and kicked me in the kishkas."

"What are you talking about?" Sally blurted.

"You think you have problems? You should try mine on for size. Like I told you, you don't strike me as conventionally crazy. What's more, for what Tom's opinion is worth—no, that's unfair because it's worth a great deal. Point is, he wouldn't commit himself outright but if he didn't three-quarters agree with me he'd have snorted and marched off with instructions to dump you in the nearest hospital at once. Follow me?"

"Uh . . . He does seem like a fairly direct sort of person."

"Direct? You don't know the half of it. He can go from blunt to caustic to get lost in less time than anybody else I ever met. Must be why I like him so much. I tend to drift off like a hot-air balloon into private worlds of my own, and I rely on Tom to create ballast and put my feet back on Mother Earth. Which, as I was going to say, seems to be where your feet are, even though your head has gone somewhere else entirely." He shivered visibly. "Sherlock Holmes he say, sling out what's impossible and whatever's left over must be true. But what do you do when the bit that's over is impossible too?"

"Nick, damn you!" Sally cried. "Stop dropping these tantalizing hints! Come to the bloody *point!*"

"I don't know whether I have a point to come to," he retorted. "What I've hit on isn't so much an explanation as a ridiculous fantasy."

"I don't give a damn what you call it, I want to hear it anyhow."

Nick sighed. "Very well. It occurs to me that if your visions aren't simply generated by an over-fertile and somewhat deranged imagination, they could be elegantly accounted for by assuming that what you see is life on other worlds."

XIV

She sat there, eyes wide and mouth ajar, for long moments. In the end, her voice quavering, she said, "Oh, that's absurd!"

"As a matter of fact, it isn't, and there's the hell of it." Nick chuckled. "Obviously there's never been on Earth a race of bald people with ears like snakes', nor marauding barbarians with four arms apiece, let alone intelligent vegetables living inside mountains which use human beings to plant out their young. So . . ." He took a swig of wine. "Oh, it'll probably turn out all these visions stem from some collection of science fiction stories you read as a kid."

"If you didn't mean me to take it seriously," she complained, "why mention the idea?"

He hesitated. "For a moment," he admitted at length, "I did mean it to be taken seriously."

"But I thought there couldn't possibly be life on the planets. Venus and Mercury are too hot, Mars is too cold, Jupiter is too big—isn't that right?"

"Interesting," he said, cocking one eyebrow. "I wonder what you studied at school, what your hobbies were, what you used to do for a living before you—ah—forgot. . . . But you're only half right. I'm not talking about planets of our solar system. I mean planets of other stars. Maybe even of double stars like the one in your latest vision, though most scientists think that's the least likely place for life to evolve. Myself, I'm inclined to disagree; the extremes of climate might even accelerate the evolution of intelligence by applying the right kind of stress. However that may be, it's certain that there must be other intelligent species in our galaxy. All those billions of stars, some of them very much like our sun. . . . I said I believe in the law of chance. It states there must be hundreds of thousands of planets as habitable as Earth."

"But how could memories of other planets get into my head?" she exclaimed, and was at once fearful of being overheard. She dropped her voice. "And. I am absolutely convinced they *are* memories. At any rate they're in the part of my mind where memories feel as though they probably belong. They aren't in the least like what one conjures up in the imagination."

"I suppose it's conceivable," Nick said, looking past her into nowhere, "that while we concentrate on what seem to us the most logical means of long-distance communication—radio, particularly—some other species may employ techniques we've barely dreamed of. Maybe there really is such a thing as thought-transference. Maybe it really is independent of natural limitations which we mistakenly believe to be absolute, like the speed of light. Oh, hell!" he said with sudden annoyance. "I know I'm likely to wake up tomorrow and decide I ought to laugh at myself, but right now the whole lot is hanging together and giving me all sorts of spin-off. I told you I have a gift for extracting patterns from random-looking data. Well, I just spotted one."

"Tell me!" Sally leaned eagerly toward him.

"Well . . . OK. One thing does strike me about all the episodes you've described. Each of them climaxed at a moment when you were close to death, except the one where you saw yourself as a bride. Even that could be made to fit if . . . Well, suppose you weren't going to be married to a real husband, but to a deity? In other words, sacrificed?"

"Nick, I can't believe it, but you've done it again." She clenched her fists and closed her eyes for a second. "Yes, that has to be right. It wasn't just happiness I was feeling. It was more like religious ecstasy. And I mentioned I'd been given a cupful of something sour that I was compelled to swallow—or did I? No, I think I left that out. But that's the way it was, and when I'd drunk the stuff I couldn't care what became of me."

She hesitated. "You seem to be talking about some sort of—well—reincarnation."

"To be candid, I don't know whether I'm talking about anything. I can think of one way of finding out, though. Do you recall the night sky from any of these visions clearly enough to draw the constellations? I have a friend who's an astronomer, and it's barely possible he could figure out whether what you saw is a transform of known star-patterns, viewed from a different point in space."

Sally shook her head. "I'm sorry, but I'm sure I couldn't remember a nighttime scene clearly enough."

"Pity."

Depressed, they sat in silence for a while. The waiter offered dessert, which they refused in favor of coffee. Eventually Sally had to stifle a yawn, and Nick glanced at her.

"Hmm! I was going to suggest calling by at the nearest police station—wasn't that the original plan? But by the look of you, you're sleepy, and no wonder. You've had a tiring day. Want me to put you up and take you to the police in the morning instead? I doubt if they could do much at this time of night anyway."

"If I won't be too much trouble."

"No, you aren't *trouble*. You're *puzzle,* and that's an altogether different thing. Waiter, the bill, please!"

They walked back arm in arm, saying little. It had clouded over while they were in the restaurant, and obviously there had been a brief shower; wet paving stones were giving back their reflections to the street-lamps. But it was dry again now, if somewhat cool.

"You know, in spite of everything," Sally murmured, "I am very happy. I never thought I'd be happy again."

"Wish I could be," was Nick's caustic answer. "But I

foresee a sleepless night. My brain is full of things I want to believe and in good conscience can't. Oh, shut up, Jenkins. You're talking nonsense."

"But I like hearing you talk."

"I hate what I want to talk about," he grunted, and no more was said until they reached Mulborough Square.

For the fourth time since leaving Mamble Row Clyde West sat in the home of one of his friends, admiring the children, accepting a couple of drinks, taking a circuitous route to the subject he was concerned with: can you put me up for a while?

For the fourth time he found his story about being evicted didn't hold water, and for the fourth time he had to say wearily, "Sure, sure, I know, I know" as his friends held forth authoritatively on the law which meant he couldn't just be turned out on the street.

But he dared not explain the real story behind his request. It was just too—too *incredible*.

He had drunk a lot more than he should have done, and eaten nothing bar a sandwich offered at the second place he visited. When he left the fourth, late and in disgust, he was resigned to the fact that, short of booking into an expensive hotel room or sitting up all night in a club, he would have to go back to the Rowalls' house and take his chances.

Putting off that moment as long as possible, he wandered dismally along trying to figure out an alternative. Suddenly he realized he was only a few blocks from the square where Nick Jenkins lived.

Alcohol combined with annoyance to spawn inspiration.

"The bastard landed me in this mess," he muttered to the air. "OK. I did him the favor he wanted. He can bloody well do me one in return!"

Having passed a pleasant evening with Gemma, Tom Gospell returned her early to the nurses' hostel where she lodged; she had to be on duty again tomorrow.

Getting back in his car, he realized he had omitted to keep his promise and phone Nick about his findings. They amounted effectively to nothing, but even negative evidence . . .

You know, given the state that girl was in, maybe I ought to call personally instead of phoning.

He glanced at his watch. It was still quite early by Nick's standards—Nick had always been a night bird—and anyhow his route took him close to Mulborough Square.

Making up his mind, Tom started the engine.

"Here they come!" Alfred Rowall hissed, leaning down to the driver's window of Terry Jones's car, which had been parked for the past hour and a half close to Nick's home.

"Not before bloody time," the driver grunted. "You're going to square with me for every penny of lost business, you know. Sunday night's one of my best times!"

"You keep your mouth shut and do as you're told," Alfred retorted. "I hope that character you brought along is as good as you said. If he isn't . . ."

"Oh, hell," Terry sighed. "Yes, yes, and yes again. You asked for the best muscle-man on the manor, I got him for you—and that won't come cheap, either, especially if he lets it slip to his boss that he's taken on outside work. Still, that's your worry; I just laid him on for you. You better get to bloody action stations if you're going to."

"On my way," Alfred said. "You know . . ." He curled his lip. "You know, this is quite like the old days in Soho."

"When you've finished bloody reminiscing—!"

"OK, OK!"

Exactly how it happened, Nick Jenkins never remembered. He and Sally had just drawn abreast of the entrance to his home, and he was fishing for his front-door key, when—

An explosion of pain behind his head sent him stumbling against the shadowed steps of the house's porch. There was a cry, in Sally's voice he thought, but it was instantly stifled. He was vaguely aware of being hit a second time, even harder, and of unfriendly paving stones rising to meet him.

At the same time there were noises: a car revving up, approaching, squealing to a halt very close to him. He was making a noise himself, but it felt muffled, more like the thought of a call for help than the actual cry. His giddy vision informed him of someone (Sally?) being carted bodily past him, but he himself was grappling with—failing to match—overwhelmed by a great brawny man whose face was as inhuman as that of a creature from one of Sally's visions. It seemed like a tremendous mental achivement to be able to tell himself that the attacker must be wearing a nylon stocking as a mask.

And another thought dominated everything else:

Shit. People can be knocked unconscious. I never had it happen before but it's happening now. . . .

All of a sudden, there was a cry, followed by confused shouts. Someone, not close, shouted, "Hey! What the—?"

Someone else exclaimed, "Get out of here, fast!"

Another voice, seeming familiar: "You can't just dump him like that—"

Another: "The hell you say! You've got what you bloody wanted, and I'm going!"

(Car engine roaring.)

Nausea, and pain, and utter indescribable defeat.

XV

Concepts welled up:

To be trapped—to be ambushed—to be taken by surprise . . .

They evoked echoes.

Something had been put over Sally's mouth before she could utter the cry for help which she intended. Her gasp for breath had brought with it fumes, and rapid oblivion.

But perhaps, as much as passing out from—whatever it was—the stuff, she had simply fainted. For she seemed to be recovering consciousness remarkably quickly. She could neither move, even to open her eyes, nor speak, but she could register sensations: being picked up and set down, people exchanging words in angry voices, warmth, weakness.

Links with reality, hungrily seized on: the car rocking as it turned corners too fast, exterior noise which she recognized including a blast of music from a bar, and—so on. She was muddled. Things weren't going into the right places in her mind.

A familiar sensation.

Familiar?

I know those voices: Alfred and Bella. And someone else, and . . .

"No, I won't, damn it!" A man, near hysteria. "You never told me what it was all about! 'Settle a score,' that's what you said! But this is bloody *kidnapping*!"

"Ah, shut up!"

Pause. Someone had hold of her, very tightly. There was sweat gathering at the place where skin touched skin.

"All right, here you are!" In the same near-hysterical tone. "And you pay up tomorrow or I swear you'll wish you'd never been born! Out—*quickly!*"

"All clear." That was Bella. "Hurry."

"You remember what I said!"

"Of course you'll be paid! *Buzz off!*"

The smell was recognizable: the smell of the Rowalls' home, stale and tainted as though fresh air had been a stranger here for decades. She writhed at that, but it was useless. She lacked strength to break free.

"In here," Bella said. Sally felt herself thrown down on a bed with a sagging spring.

"She's starting to come to!" Alfred exclaimed.

"Soon fix that. . . ."

Bella's practiced hands lashing her wrists and ankles, for all her weak resistance. A coarse cloth forced into her mouth by way of a gag.

"This time there's going to be no mistake." Bella. "I'll get Richard here right away. Sort out everything."

"But we weren't supposed to—"

"That's what has to be done. She'll be safe for the time being." A final check of the knots; it wasn't rope she had used, but something more like electrical cord. "OK, get on with it."

Door shut. Temporary silence. Unspeakable loneliness. Sally's mistreated mind dissolved into—into . . .

Loneliness a little less than total. Granted, she was the sole inhabitant of this isolated planetoid, but when she looked out at the frozen vastness of the sky she could gaze yonder at a blue sun and think of the Chidnim who basked in its warmth, yonder at an orange one and picture the Tansules at play, overhead at a pure white one and remind herself that was the orb shining on the cities of the Iark.

It was a vast temptation to forget, however, that

those suns were not the only ones in this area of the galaxy, and that the planetoid's sluggish rotation would in a few hours show her others, nearer, falling prey to the hordes of the Yem.

As for her own people . . . Between her and home stretched light-year on empty light-year of interstellar space, as implacably—as inhumanly—hostile as the Yem themselves. Nothing sheltered her from the enmity of either except the shell of this observation station.

When her predicament laid siege to her mental defenses it was time to lose herself in routine tasks. She did so now, moving to survey her instrument panels. Catching sight of her reflection in a polished dial, she cocked her head in a manner that had attracted many a masculine eye, and spent a brief moment admiring her pure green complexion, the symmetrical patterns of the scales on her face, the litheness of her neck and arms.

A modicum of reassurance was always welcome. . . .

More cheerful, she continued to the next panel and checked the readings. She felt a pang of intense cold, as though she had been sprayed with liquid air.

"Surely not me!" she heard herself say to the heedless void. "Surely not me, not here!"

For life seemed suddenly very sweet for its own sake, too precious to be wasted on the desert of space.

Yet the instruments' message was unequivocal. The harsh truth lowered at her. Lights and gauges spoke wordlessly of a swarm of Yem-spawn spreading outward and onward in another gigantic seeding; they spoke of many which had passed close enough to this lonely planetoid to detect that here she was.

The Yem-spawn had turned, like sailboats tacking on the radiation-wind. They lacked the consciousness which would warn them that there was only one of her, and their second generation would die on sterile rock. They were stooping on their quarry. Nothing would deflect their course now.

Her slender agile arms reached for controls; her green shining hands glinted iridescently in the lights.

*There was a final service she could perform for her
people: transmit the signal stating that another swarm
was on its way.*

*And by implication that they would have to establish
another forward observation post in place of this one.*

*She spoke swiftly to an image, and received condo-
lences which rang unintentionally hollow. She knew,
as did the other, that her position was hopeless; the
evolutionary brilliance of the Yem had once more
pierced their most ingenious defenses. . . .*

*Then she went to the transparent door of the dome
and looked out one last time at the stars.*

*The Tansules' sun blurred and wavered. There came
the spawn. Clawing a path along the distortions of space
in a manner so subtle her own people had as yet only
defined it, not comprehended it, they were exulting in
the discovery, somewhere nearby, of another species
suitable for their future reproduction.*

*She waited until she actually saw the swarm ground,
knowing that afterward its members would be helpless
to return to the spaceways, and then blew the air out
of the dome.*

*Her last thought was of the baffled less-than-con-
sciousness of the Yem stopping—not dying, for they
were not yet fully alive. Stopping. Then thought stopped
too.*

Sally wanted to cry. That creature had been so
beautiful—so graceful—so . . . !

The word was, had to be: *human.*

In every way that counted. Never mind scales, green
skin, incredible tallness, thinness, angularity such as
might be dreamed of by an Earthly dancer and never
attained—that was a person!

To think of such loveliness being wasted on the im-
personal dark filled Sally with boundless misery.

And yet that beauty was not altogether gone, for
she—a stranger, an unknown—remembered it.

How?

Desperate, Sally Ercott groped toward knowledge

of a tremendous truth, while the enemy fumed and fought and struggled to prevent her, and in the nick of time, as it viewed things, interrupted.

The door of the room opened, shut, was locked with a click. What room? She forced one eyelid ajar, and recognized what she had only glimpsed before: the Rowalls' bedroom. And here was Alfred, and—

And his hand tearing from her body the T-shirt Nick had loaned her: rip—rip—rags.

What the hell ...?

Tom Gospell's mind had been more on where there might be a space to park his car, here at Mulborough Square, than on anything else. Abruptly he caught sight of a figure in the beam of his headlight. A black man on the sidewalk bending over somebody else, either holding him down or—well, perhaps trying to help him up, but in either case . . .

Tom leaned out of his window. "What's going on?" he barked in his most authoritative voice.

An answer came back from the black man. "Ah, you tell me! But this guy got hit over the head. Better call an ambulance."

Tom heaved a sigh, set his handbrake, and climbed out of the over-small car. "Let's have a look at him," he said reflexively. "I'm a doctor—Damnation! Nick!"

He dashed forward and dropped on one knee.

"You know him?" the black man said, sounding foggy, as though he too had been attacked.

"Yes! Do you?"

"Sure, met him today at lunchtime in a pub . . . . Is he OK?"

"I'm OK!" Nick managed to say, and brushing aside Tom's arm, staggered to his feet, gingerly touching the back of his neck. "But what counts is—Tom?" In a tone of sudden incredulity.

"Yes! What *happened?* Don't tell me the girl went for you!"

"No!"—and simultaneously, "No!" They both spoke at once. Nick reacted, turning.

"Who—? But you're Clyde West that I met earlier. . . . Oh, God. What can possibly be going on around here? It's—it's insane, the whole shooting match is *crazy!*"

He swayed a little. Tom caught him by the arm.

"Now you look here, Nick," he said in a gruff voice. "You take it slowly and explain exactly what happened. Come on." Fishing out his miniature flashlight with his spare hand, he played its beam over Nick, looking for major injuries.

"I don't know what happened," Nick sighed. "Someone jumped me, and I think someone made off with Sally, and . . . and I didn't see any more."

"I did," Clyde said. "I—Oh, the hell with why I was coming this way, but I was. And just as I rounded the corner I saw the whole thing. There was this car waiting, Terry Jones's car, and him—Nick—and this girl Sally, they were just kind of pausing before going up these steps, and a guy I don't know appeared out of the shadows with a blackjack and two people went off with Sally, bundled her into the car. I did try to stop them, honest, but I was right back there." He gestured vaguely along the street.

Tom drew a deep breath. "Let me get this straight. You arrived just in time to see Nick and Sally being attacked by people from—from a car that belonged to who?"

"Terry Jones," Clyde said. "Friend of Alfred and Bella Rowall."

"How do you know?"

"Ah, *shit!* It's his own car, a Cortina, got this sign on top belongs to a rented-car company he works for, sort of free-lance. If it wasn't his then the company's acquired another driver with the same model!" Clyde added by way of a topper, *"And* bent the same corner at the back end! Saw when it drove off the nearside rear light's broken!"

"And they took Sally with them?" Nick demanded, straightening.

"Sure as hell did! I interrupted before they got tight

hold of you, or likely you'd have been dragged aboard with her!"

"Nick—" Tom began. Nick cut him short.

"We've got to get after the Rowalls. This minute! Tom, don't argue, for pity's sake. I honestly believe—I swear I believe—it's not just Sally who's in danger, but the planet Earth."

# XVI

There had been a brief confused argument with Nick:

"No, my Jag is a sight faster—"

"Idiot, who can drive that fast in London traffic? Anyhow mine has room for four people—"

"If we take the top down so does—"

"Want to waste time on that job if half what you say is true?"

It all seemed to be over in just enough time for Clyde West to realize he was drunker than he'd imagined. But it didn't last quite long enough for him to voice the suggestion he had in mind, that he should not—please not, under any circumstances—come with them. Mamble Row was the last place he wanted to be taken to, and in any case, wouldn't it be sensible if one of them went to a phone, called the police, brought reinforcements—?

No use. Somehow he was in the back seat of Tom Gospell's cramped Mini, doors were slamming, tires were squealing, and Nick was issuing urgent directions. They had gone half a mile before he managed to ask, "Nick, when you get there, what do you want to *do?*"

"No idea," was the answer. "But something's got to be done. Let's work out what it is when it happens!"

"Next on the left?" Tom said.

"Next but one," Nick told him. "Careful, it's a narrow street. Pull up immediately after you turn the corner."

Street-lamps came and went; it was a dead time of night in this part of London. The pubs and cinemas had long ago shut, and since it was Sunday only a few buses and cars were on the road. It had made for a fast trip.

But—!

Halting the car opposite Number 5 Mamble Row, Tom discovered with a wrenching sense of dislocation that he had been carried this far not by what Nick had said but by the tone of urgency in which he had said it.

The planet Earth in danger . . . ? Lord, could that girl's delusions be infectious?

He stared across the street. The house was quiet, all its windows in darkness bar two on the entrance floor. No light shone through the glass panes set into the front door.

Nick had already piled out and was holding his seat out of Clyde's way. He said, "Got your door key with you?"

"Yes," the Jamaican muttered. Plainly he was not happy at being involved in this any more than Tom was.

"Nick, what *are* you going to do?" Tom demanded, leaving the car with equal reluctance.

"Get Sally out of there and raise as much hell as I can."

"But why?"

"I told you!"

"You gave me some sort of double-talk." Tom caught at his friend's arm. "Don't you think it would be better to wait until we can get the police here? I mean, there are two witnesses to Sally being kidnapped, you and Clyde, and—"

"Oh, hell!" Nick tore his arm loose. "OK, you go phone the fuzz! I want to get into that house this minute!"

Urging Clyde to hurry, he dashed across the street.

After a moment's irresolute delay, Tom heaved a sigh and followed.

Kick up enough row and someone will call the police without being asked. Besides, if there's trouble, an extra pair of hands will be useful. . . . But I wish to God Nick would take my advice occasionally. He didn't have to get mixed up in this. Idiot!

They stole up the front steps of the house. After some fumbling—he had sobered up considerably, but now he was shaking with apprehension—Clyde managed to slip his key into the lock.

"Turn it gently," Nick hissed. "Don't make a noise when you open it."

Clyde muttered something which might have been, "Think I have to be told?" And very cautiously swung the door wide.

There was no sign of anybody in the dark hallway or on the staircase at the far end. But a line of light showed under each of the two doors at left and right.

"What are these rooms?" Nick whispered.

"The Rowalls' bedroom on the right," Clyde answered equally softly. "Living room on the left. Has a door to the kitchen off it, and there's another door at the back of the hall." He pointed.

Standing anxiously in the porchway, Tom watched as Nick crept silently to set his ear against the bedroom door. He shook his head, and moved to the living room.

He returned on tiptoe.

"I think I heard someone in the living room, but not talking, just moving on a chair. Where's Sally's room?"

"Second floor right."

"OK. I'll creep up and see if I can hear anything. You two stay put, make sure nobody can get out. Is there a rear exit?"

"Door into a backyard," Clyde whispered. "But you can't get out of the yard unless you climb over a high wooden fence, and that's old and rotten."

"What about the basement?"

"Never saw anyone go down to it. Door to it is under the stairs but it's always kept locked. The windows are blocked with bits of board, so you can't look in."

"OK. Tom!" Beckoning urgently. "Come in and shut the door!"

Reluctantly Tom complied, despite his bulk doing so soundlessly. Nick turned and started up the stairs, using the outside edge of the treads to minimize the risk of a board creaking under his weight. Outside a car drew to a halt. From next door, through a cardboard-thin wall, there came the faint sound of a TV playing. Otherwise everything was very still.

Nick had almost reached the first landing when— *R-r-r-ring!* Someone leaned angrily on the doorbell. At once there were footsteps in the living room, the door was flung open, and Bella Rowall switched on the hallway light.

She found herself face to face with Clyde West.

Instantly, as though overtaken by uncontrollable rage, her expression became a mask of hate.

"You stinking meddlesome son of a bitch!" she roared, and launched herself bodily at him.

Taken completely by surprise, Clyde had no chance to fend off the attack. He was bowled over with a yell, and Bella flung herself on top of him as though determined to batter and claw him to death.

"Hey!" a voice said through the front door. "What the hell is going on?"

But neither Nick nor Tom paid any attention. They converged on Bella, who had clamped her hands around Clyde's throat and seemed set on strangling him. From between her bared teeth issued filthy insults interspersed with drops of spittle.

Overhead a lock clicked, a board creaked. Slow light steps descended the stairs.

Nick and Tom seized Bella's arms, but—seeming possessed of superhuman strength—she fended them off, releasing her clutch on Clyde's neck and swinging and kicking wildly. A lucky sweep of one leg knocked Nick momentarily off balance, and she rounded on Tom, screaming. He tried to catch and pinion her arms, but she was so fast and so improbably strong he missed, trapping only the shoulder-strap of her dress, which tore to the waist, revealing her gross bosom packed into her brassiere—and something else.

"What the—?" Nick said softly, and then with sudden energy he hurled himself forward, first poised to swing with all his force at the small of her back. The blow connected. Bella convulsed, uttering a scream, and within another few seconds the combined efforts of Nick, Tom, and Clyde contrived to pinion her to the floor. She lay there, mouth ajar, seeming to be in mortal agony.

"What's that on her back?" Clyde whispered.

"That" began below her shoulder blades, where the skin of her back united with something smooth and a little shiny, like wet leather. It was grayish-green under the single overhead bulb, and it pulsed a little. It was at least eight inches across and roughly lozenge-shaped. In texture it resembled a bladder filled with half-melted grease.

The doorbell rang again, accompanied this time by furious knocking. They ignored it, staring with nausea at the foul growth.

"My God," Clyde whispered. "And to think men can bear to touch a woman with a thing like that on her!"

Tom gathered himself. He said, "Hard to believe, isn't it? But some men go for women with—uh—abnormalities." Cautiously, for fear she might again try to break free, he produced from his pocket a pen which he poised over the gray-green surface. He prodded; the thing seemed to try to writhe away.

"Any idea what it is?" Nick muttered.

"No, one. It's not a cancer, or a birthmark, or anything I ever saw before."

"I think I know what it is," Nick said after a pause. They were talking in normal tones now, against the racket from the door.

"What?" Tom glanced at him, surprised.

"I think it's what's been—uh—driving Bella Rowall."

The other two stared at him incredulously. Before either could speak again, however, there was a shrill scream from the staircase, and they glanced up to see Mrs. Ramsay, wearing an old dressing gown and down-at-heel slippers and carrying a poker. Her eyes goggled as they took in the sight of her landlady being held down on the hall floor by three men.

"Police!" she shrieked. "Help! Rape! Murder!"

"Madam, there's no cause for alarm," Tom boomed in his most magisterial voice. "I'm a doctor, and this lady has had some kind of fit."

"Lies! Lies!" Mrs. Ramsay cried. "The doctor's on the doorstep and you won't let him in! *Police!*"

There was a window on the half-landing of the staircase. Catching sight of it, she stumbled toward it and smashed it with her poker.

"Help! *He-e-elp!*"

"Doctor on the doorstep," Nick breathed. "Very interesting! You two hang on tight." He jumped to his feet and hurried along the hallway.

"Dr. Argyle, I presume," he said as he opened up. Confronted by this stranger, the visitor—who was a thin man of late middle age with a peaked, ill-tempered face, carrying a medical bag—blinked several times, caught sight of Bella, and at once turned to run off. Nick caught him by the coat-sleeve.

"*Oh* no you don't," he said, dragging Argyle over the threshold, pushing him into the hallway, closing the door, and setting his back against it. "You've got questions to answer, chum. Like what that growth is on Bella Rowall's back, and what sort of so-called sedatives you've been pumping into a girl called Sally Ercott!"

Argyle stared blankly at him for a long moment. Then he unexpectedly let fall his bag and buried his face in his hands.

"I'll keep an eye on this bastard," Nick said. "Tom, think you can hold Bella down by yourself?"

"Oh, I've got a firm grip now and my full weight on her," Tom grunted.

"Right. Clyde, go find something to tie her up with." And he added in an ironical shout to Mrs. Ramsay, "Madam, keep it up, please—you're doing a fine job. The sooner the police get here, the better!"

Mrs. Ramsay, hysterical, shattered another pane of glass and went on yelling.

XVII

Chief Inspector Dougherty, yawning enormously, hung up his jacket and sat down on the edge of the bed to remove his shoes.

The phone rang.

He ignored it. But it went right on ringing, and eventually his wife—who was already in bed—hissed at him to hurry up and answer before the noise woke the children.

Furious, he plodded out of the room.

"Chief, this is Bray!" the sergeant's voice said excitedly. "We just got report from Mamble Row!"

"Bloody *hell!*" Dougherty said. "Am I never going to get a night's sleep again? What kind of bloody report?"

"Hedger was just handing over to Prior when they spotted this hire-car, the one belonging to the man Terry Jones, stopping at the Rowalls' place. That was—uh—about twenty minutes ago. The Rowalls got out and went indoors, half carrying somebody who looked very much like the girl who's been lodging there. Hedger swears it was her, and she couldn't walk unaided—seemed to be drugged or something. Drunk maybe, but . . . Anyhow: next thing that happened, we got a report from the phone-tap people. Bella said some very interesting things to Dr. Argyle, including threats that indicate she has a powerful hold over him. I'd play you the tape but I think you may not want to waste the time. Because she ordered him to come over right away. Said the dope he gave her before was no damn good and she wants something which can be relied on to keep the girl quiet for at least twenty-four hours. Argyle said it might kill her, and Bella said the hell with that, never mind, just so long as she—Hang on, sir. I have another call coming in from Prior."

A pause. Then: "Hey! There was another car arrived at Mamble Row, and the registration matches the one belonging to the doctor who was at Jenkins' place earlier. And one of the passengers sounds like Jenkins himself, and another could be the Jamaican, West, who's lodging with the Rowalls."

Dougherty hesitated a fraction of a second. Then he said crisply, "OK, spring the trap!"

"Both places?" Bray said eagerly.

"Yes, Soho too. I'll go straight to Mamble Row in my own car."

He slammed down the phone and lumbered back into the bedroom for his shoes and coat.

Stan Hedger should long ago have left the Mamble Row watch-post, but after all this time he wasn't going to miss the climax when it happened. Jubilantly he cradled the phone over which he had just heard the news.

"Action stations!" he informed Bob Prior.

Eyes glued to the binoculars, Prior retorted, "You'd better get into action yourself, then, if the whole operation isn't to be wasted."

"What?"

"There must be a hell of a racket over there. People are turning on lights in the next house, raising their windows, leaning out and shouting. . . . We'll have the uniform boys there any moment."

"Christ, that could ruin everything!" Hedger blurted. "You better raise Information Room, get a message through to hold it!"

He ran pell-mell for the door. But by the time he dashed out of the front entrance of the building, he knew he was too late, for a howling police car was that minute turning into Mamble Row. Shouting, waving, was useless; long before he caught up they had arrived at Number Five and were authoritatively demanding admission.

Bloody hell, thought Stan Hedger. *The chief just won't be fit to live with after this. . . . Still, I'd better see what I can salvage.*

Knocking and ringing. Argyle took an immense grip on himself and restored his manner to a sort of pathetic dignity. Nick turned and undid the lock.

"Officer, come on in!" he invited. "Not before time, either."

On the doorstep two uniformed constables blinked at the spectacle before them: a burly man with a beard kneeling across the legs of a half-naked woman while a black man strapped her wrists behind her back with adhesive tape, and on the half-landing of the staircase another much older woman brandishing a poker in one hand, clinging to the banister with another, trying to go on screaming but clearly too hoarse now.

"What—in the world—is going on?" the first of the constables said, diffidently stepping across the threshold and looking very much as though he wished he'd never joined the force.

"Ah, officer!" Tom said, and added for the latest of several times today, "I'm a doctor. It's quite all right —come on in!"

"Liar!" moaned Mrs. Ramsay from the stairs, and gasped for breath.

"I *am* a doctor," Argyle said in a thin voice. He bent to reclaim his bag. "Whatever that person may say. I was telephoned about half an hour ago by the lady who is at present being tied up. I don't know who these people are, I don't believe they have any legal right to be in this house, and I would suggest that you take them into custody at once before they can assault anybody else!" He set his chin at a determined angle.

"What's happening?" a voice called from the street. The second constable shouted back, "It's like a

bloody circus up here! But you better get another car.
Looks like we'll be taking a few people in. And make
that an ambulance too while you're about it."

"Oh, I don't think there's any need for that," Argyle
said quickly. "Once the lady is released—"

During this exchange Nick, Tom, and Clyde had
been staring at each other. Suddenly Nick managed
a grin, and the others responded. In its way, the situation
was rather comical.

"I got her," Clyde muttered to Tom. "Think it might
be a good idea if you—uh—stood on your dignity,
hm?"

Tom nodded, rising to his feet like a hippopotamus
rising from its wallow:

"This person, I gather, claims to be a medical
practitioner?" he said, gesturing at Argyle. "And this
woman is alleged to be a patient of his?"

"Yes!" Argyle blustered. "And what you've done to
her is unforgivable! Absolutely unforgivable!"

"In that case," Tom murmured, "tell the officers what
treatment you've been giving her for the—ah—back
condition she suffers from. Come to that, tell them
what it's called."

He stood aside, pointing at Bella. "See it, officer?"
he added.

The first constable's eyes bulged. His mouth worked
as though he were fighting the urge to vomit. Behind
him his companion looked up, shut his eyes instantly,
and unashamedly turned away, uttering a sound like
"ugh!"

"I'm waiting!" Tom rapped. "What's the medical
name for that condition? What are the proprietary
names of the drugs you've been administering?"

"I—I . . ." Argyle put his hand to his head and
swayed.

"There, officer!" Tom said in triumph. "That's someone who ought to be in custody! Posing as a doctor—
can't even name the condition Mrs. Rowall suffers
from—can't or won't tell us what treatment he's pre-
scribed. . . . *Hah!*"

Confused, the constables mutely glanced at one another, and came up with no bright ideas.

Sensing that things were going their way, Nick said, "And now we've sorted that out, perhaps you'd ask this so-called doctor about the treatment he's been giving a girl lodging in this house, a girl called Sally Ercott suffering from acute amnesia who ought to have been in a hospital long ago—"

"I don't want to know about that," the first constable broke in. "You lot, all of you, are coming to the station with us. Do your arguing there! Get that stuff off the woman you've tied up!" he added to Clyde. "We'll put her in the ambulance when it shows up and she can be looked after properly. A doctor who can't name the disease, another whose idea of proper treatment is to knock her down and tie her up—Christ, this is a madhouse!"

Another siren bellowed in the distance, drawing closer.

Nick clenched his fists. "But wait a second!" he exclaimed desperately. "There's a girl here who's been bloody kidnapped! I saw it happen—I got hit over the head myself—and Mr. West here is also a witness!"

The constable curled his lip.

"You tell all that to the station sergeant," he said. "Come on, move. There's the ambulance"—jerking his thumb over his shoulder as a large white vehicle drew up—"so there's no more call to worry."

"Wouldn't surprise me if this lot needed a hospital more than a cell," the second policeman said caustically. "Right, *move!*"

"Hold everything!"

A shout, as a blazer-clad fresh-faced young man came panting into view. "Now what is it?" the first officer muttered wearily.

"Detective-Constable Hedger," the newcomer forced out, producing a warrant card from his pocket. "Covert Squad!"

He came up the steps to the front door two at a time, surveyed the situation, and gave an approving nod.

"Ah, you got Mrs. Rowall. Good work!" With a nod to Tom. "How about her husband? We don't want him to fade into the woodwork, you know."

"I'll be damned!" Nick took half a step toward him. "If I'd known who was following us I'd never have shaken you off—I'd have said come and join the conversation, quick! Do you know what's become of Sally Ercott?"

"I'm afraid not. Ah . . . you do mean the slim blonde who was with you tonight, who's been lodging here the past five going on six weeks?"

"Yes! Look, Mr.—uh—Hedger, how did you get involved in all this?"

"Oh, we've had this place under twenty-four-hour surveillance for weeks now," Hedger said mildly. And was interrupted. There was a roar of engines from the street, the sound of at least a half dozen cars. Astonished, they saw one after another draw up and a score of men in plain clothes pile out to take station covering the house.

"Christ," said the second constable. "I wish I'd known we were letting ourselves in for this lot. It's *big!*"

Hedger gave a modest cough. "That's the Squad arriving," he explained unnecessarily. "Chief Inspector Dougherty is on his way with a search warrant, and we'll get this whole thing sorted out."

He glanced at Argyle. "Aren't you Dr. Argyle? I've been wondering how you tie in with this lot. I look forward with great interest to hearing your—"

There was a faint whimpering cry from inside the Rowalls' bedroom. Nick swung around.

"*Sally!*"

He rattled the handle of the door, but it was locked from inside. "Hedger!" he barked. "Help me break it down!"

"Well, sir, strictly we ought to wait for—"

"Tom!"

The doctor needed no urging. He hurled his full

weight against the door and the lock splintered from the old dry frame. Almost falling over him, Nick rushed into the room at his heels, and saw—

· And saw—

It was no use. It was purely impossible. It couldn't be happening. Not something so loathsome, so revolting, so nauseating. . . .

Sally, stripped to the waist, laid bound and gagged on the bed. Seated with his back to her, Alfred Rowall, likewise half-naked, his knees doubled up, his arms clasped around them, his head forward resting on his wrists.

And from his spine, reaching up like a blind snake, *growing* like a plant-shoot rooted in a duplicate of the gray-green horror they had seen on Bella's body, a sort of tendril, weaving back and forth, extending now to brush against, stick to, Sally's fair pale skin exactly on the line of her backbone.

 XVIII

Nick took one long stride and with his clubbed forearm hit Alfred Rowall so hard behind the head he simply fell straight over, lay inert for a second—and opened his eyes and mouth as wide as they would go and began to scream with eldritch shrillness and agonizing violence, as though he were in more pain than a human body was designed to endure.

The tendril from the thing on his back seemed to search the air for what had been intended as its target; finding none, it began to shrink back into itself.

Nick paid no attention. Bending over Sally, he satisfied himself there was no worse mark on her than a little redness, as though the spot had been touched with a brush dipped in acid. Then with one hand he rolled her on her back, with the other tugged a penknife from his pocket and attacked the flex which bound her.

She seemed at best semiconscious. She opened her eyes long enough to recognize him, then let the lids fall again while he finished freeing her and extracting the gag from her mouth.

"Sally, are you all right?" he demanded, loud over the incessant screaming of Alfred Rowall. And added over his shoulder to Tom, "Can't you shut that bastard up somehow?"

Tom looked dubious for a second, but it was obvious that Rowall was in mortal torment; he was writhing now and going into convulsions, arms and legs flailing.

"Mr. Hedger, get me Argyle's medical bag," he said with sudden decision. "See if there's anything in there that's fit for use."

"Get it," Hedger instructed, as Nick helped Sally to turn around and put her feet on the floor. Sitting down beside her, he put his arm around her shoulders and murmured reassurance into her ear.

"You leave that alone—it's mine!" came Argyle's angry voice from the hall, but the police commandeered his bag anyway and Hedger delivered it to Tom, who opened it and gave a loud sniff.

"Lord, he can't have cleaned and disinfected this for years!" he muttered, burrowing into the interior. "I never saw such a horrible mishmash. . . . The hell with it." He turned the bag upside down over a table and shook out the contents: almost all vials of various drugs, disposable syringes, and packs of pills.

"I knew he had a weird practice, but this beats the band." Separating the items with a distasteful finger. "That was banned last year—he has no business carrying that around either, it shouldn't be used outside a hospital ward where you can watch for side effects— that's lost its label so heaven knows what it can be. . . . Ah, some pethedrine. That'll have to do."

He filled a syringe and advanced on Rowall, who immediately began to scream even louder and strike out with arms and legs, much as Bella had done.

"Hold him down," Tom instructed, and Clyde and Hedger hurried to obey.

He poised the syringe. Then, unexpectedly, instead of sinking the needle into the man's bare arm, he plunged it into the growth on his back, at the base of the now almost retracted tendril.

From the hallway Dougherty's voice resounded. "Where's D-C Hedger? I gather he arrived ahead of the crowd!"

"Here, Chief!" Hedger called. "The room on the right!"

"Coming— Lord, what in the world is wrong with Bella Rowall's back?"

"Heaven knows, sir," was the answer in the weary tones of one of the constables who had walked ignorantly into this crisis. "We seem to have two crazy doctors, a madwoman, another old lady in hysterics—my mate took her upstairs to get over the shock and rickety though she is she managed to cop him one with a poker before we calmed her down. . . . *I* don't know, sir. You look the scene over and tell us."

"Well, I brought plenty of manpower," Dougherty said. "If you need a woman officer just shout." Entering the bedroom, he glanced around. "Ah, Hedger. And I think you're Mr. Jenkins, and you're Mr. West, and you're Dr. Gospell, and— My God! That's Alfred Rowall! What's happening to him?"

He had grown still now, lying facedown on the threadbare carpet. And the thing on his back was darkening. Shriveling. Drawing in on itself. It parted from the flesh of his body; around its edge oozed out a foul-smelling mixture of blood and some repulsive grayish liquid, the ichor of its own nature. Independently alive, it pulsated and thrust out tiny abortive pseudopods . . . and was abruptly quite still, in the middle of a great raw pit eroded out of Alfred Rowall's back. The white tips of five or six vertebrae could be clearly seen.

There was a long silence during which they all stared in pure horror, except for Sally whose eyes were closed and head was pillowed on Nick's shoulder.

The latter stirred at last and said in a gravelly voice, "I don't think it's a matter of 'what happened to Alfred Rowall?' I don't think Alfred Rowall has been Alfred Rowall for a long time. Nor, come to that, has his wife been human either."

"What nonsense is this?" Dougherty snapped. "Not human? Don't be a fool!"

"I'm telling you," Nick grunted, easing himself clear of Sally with a view to rising. "How is Bella, anyway?"

"Quiet," Clyde reported after a glance through the doorway. "Just lying there. Looks like I did a good job with that adhesive tape."

"Fine. Tom, could you take a look at Sally? I think she's in shock—either that, or they gave her something to keep her quiet. And come to think of it, the old lady upstairs must be in a pretty bad way, too."

Nodding, Tom complied, carrying out a rapid examination to which Sally listlessly consented.

"Chief Inspector," Nick said, "I gather your people have been keeping a watch on this house for some time?"

Dougherty, face darkly suspicious, nodded. "That's right. And as soon as your girlfriend feels well enough, I shall want to have a long talk with her. I suppose Rowall is dead?" he added in passing to Tom.

"Lord, yes," the doctor sighed. "Don't even have to touch him to be sure. Nobody can live with air in an open spinal canal like that. And he stopped breathing even before the—the thing withdrew."

"What is it?"

"No idea. Never seen anything like it, never heard of anything like it. . . ." To Sally he said kindly, "Lie down on your front, please, let me just take a look at that spot on your spine."

Before Dougherty could say anything else, Nick forestalled him.

"Please tell me: what made you decide to watch this house?"

"The fact that we've found one thing in common among a lot of people who've vanished recently without trace. Either they were customers of a tart who sounds a lot like Bella, over in Soho where she rents a room for—uh—professional purposes, or else they lodged here at 5 Mamble Row. Practically nobody stays in this house more than two months. And all the lodgers who've been here in the past eight months have quit after that time, gone elsewhere, and—*phfft!*"

"Wait a second," Clyde objected. "That can't be true. I mean Mrs. Ramsay up the top, she's been here for years!"

"Makes no particular odds," Dougherty replied. "She's old and half-lame, isn't she? Maybe she's no good for—for whatever they do with the people who disappear."

A look of awe spread over Clyde's face. He said in a near-whisper, "You mean I might have been the next on the list?"

With some acerbity Dougherty said, "No. The girl was to be next. You'd have been the next but one."

"You knew about this and you hadn't tried to stop it?"

"Oh, for God's sake, Mr. West! We wanted to find the people who'd already disappeared, on the one hand, and on the other figure out what the Rowalls could do to a lodger who stayed here for a while, left calmly with all his luggage and moved somewhere else and only vanished two weeks later. Right from the moment we spotted this link with the Rowalls we knew we were on to something very big indeed. We've had all kinds of wild theories ranging from slave-trading to the recruitment of spies meant to be brainwashed and returned to us with—"

"Nick!" An exclamation from Tom, bending low over Sally's back. He made a vague gesture in the direction of the table where he had emptied out Argyle's bag. "There are some tweezers there and a magnifying glass—filthy and insanitary but they'll have to do. Hurry!"

Startled, Nick rushed to obey while the others stared at Sally, mystified.

"Here!" Nick handed Tom what he wanted.

"Get a better light on this spot—bring the bedside lamp here!"

Clyde was ahead of Nick, switched it on, held it positioned over Sally.

"Got it," Tom muttered, closing the tweezers tight on—on something. Carefully he tugged . . . tugged again, a little harder . . . tugged slowly and carefully as though easing out a single thread from a densely-woven fabric. . . . "Ah," he said at last with satisfaction. "Find me something to put it in. A jar with a screw top, something like that." He held the tweezers tightly, as though afraid of dropping what he'd found.

Casting around, Nick spotted a jar which held assorted hairpins on Bella's disorderly dressing table. He tipped those out, blew away from the interior some dust, probably face powder, and offered it. Tom dropped in the mysterious object and fastened the lid tightly.

"I look forward to putting that under a microscope," he muttered.

"No, you can do better than that," Sally said, opening her eyes. It was as though removal of the object from her spine had restored her instantly to full normal consciousness. "This way!"

She jumped off the bed, heading for the door.

"Sally!" Nick hurried in her wake, peeling off his jacket to put around her naked shoulders. She ignored him completely, heading along the hallway. Arriving at the door which according to Clyde gave access to the cellar, she pushed at it. It was securely locked.

"Well, we'll try breaking the boards away from the windows," she said, turning on her heel, and this time seeming to notice Nick's proffered jacket, which she donned with a brief smile as she passed toward the front door between two rows of astonished policemen. There were more outside; there were ambulancemen demanding to know what the hell they were hanging around for; there were countless curious neighbors, either standing on their doorsteps peering toward Number 5 or leaning out of upper windows or hanging about on the fringes of the group of police.

Passing the living room door, Nick saw that Bella had been carried in there and laid on the couch, more or less facedown. The policeman who was guarding her looked extremely unhappy at leaving her bound hand and foot; however, he had plainly received no orders to release her, and she was lying quite quietly.

There was no sign of independent movement from the thing on her back. Which, it occurred to him, now had a name.

Parasite.

XIX

A rusty iron railing surrounded the "area," below street-level, on to which looked out blindly the boarded-over cellar windows.

Sally halted, gazing down.

"What's supposed to be in the cellar that's so important?" Clyde demanded, having followed close behind. "Think they hid some of their—victims down there?"

She turned a calm face to him, and spoke in tones of perfect certainty.

"No. Not that. Please could somebody tear away those boards? A crowbar or something of that kind would be useful."

"Maybe they have rescue equipment in the ambulance," Hedger suggested, and on Dougherty's nod doubled away to inquire.

The curious crowd grew ever larger as people returning home late found it impossible to park in their usual places owing to the many police cars in the narrow street, and casual passersby, spotting the commotion, wandered this way from the main street to see what the fuss was.

Dougherty called one of the Covert Squad men and instructed him to have the ends of the street closed off to both foot and vehicular traffic before it jammed solid.

Shortly Hedger returned bringing not only a crowbar but also a hatchet and a hammer, tools used for releasing people trapped in crashed cars. Together with another of the Covert Squad officers, he climbed gingerly over the railing, lowered himself into the area, and attacked the nearest boards. They must have been nailed in place long ago; they gave with the first good heave, and a faint gleam of greenish light shone from within the basement. Another couple of boards—another yet . . .

"Great God Almighty, what's *that?*" Dougherty exploded, and pointed a wavering finger.

"That's an invader from another planet," Nick said, and had to swallow hard. "Sally, am I right?"

"Yes, quite right. The adult of the creature Tom removed from my back. It's a Yem. With luck, it may be the only full-grown specimen on Earth. But we dare not bank on that." She glanced curiously at Nick. "How did you work that out? I certainly didn't tell you."

"I have a two-plus-one-and-a-half sort of mind," Nick grunted. "I get four out of things that don't add up."

Now the policemen had cleared the boards from the whole of the window. The green luminescence was as bright as embers. A stench of putrefaction assailed their nostrils. On orders from Dougherty, a large flashlight was passed down to the dismayed Hedger, who played it through the windows. Things that waved like a forest of insane ferns seemed to shrink from the light. Nick dropped on one knee for a better view.

"Christ, it's enormous!" he breathed. "It must run right back to the far wall of the house."

"This," Sally said in a didactic tone, "is not especially large. Many have been known which stretched further than the length of this street and must have weighed hundreds of tons."

"This is quite big enough to be going on with," Nick muttered, staring in horrified fascination. Inside the cellar the green-glowing alien flesh coated the floor, swelled up around the walls, draped the ceiling beams with saclike bladders and knotted, writhing hyphae. The spectacle made his skin crawl.

"It is advisable to keep away from it," Sally said to Hedger and his companion. Gratefully they scrambled back to the street.

"What—what can we do about it?" Dougherty demanded.

"Poison is the most reliable means. I would recommend obtaining a sharpened pipe at least twenty feet long, driving it into the central mass—there, you see a large lump half the height of a man toward the back of the cellar, which is the equivalent of its heart—and pumping in about two hundred gallons of undiluted hydrogen peroxide. That acts both as a cell-wall solvent and as an inhibitor for its nervous system, and kills one this size in about fifteen minutes. Fire is also fatal to it, but it has to be a hot fire and I presume you would rather not destroy the house."

"How the hell do you know all this?" Dougherty barked.

Sick of gazing at the monster, Nick straightened, and put his arm comfortingly around Sally. She was shivering. He realized belatedly that the night had turned cool.

"Let's get back indoors," he proposed. "It's chilly out here, and Sally has a long story to tell. And—uh—get the equipment she described as soon as you can."

"Where the hell am I going to get a tanker full of pure peroxide at this time of night?" Dougherty asked rhetorically, then turned away, sighing, to issue his instructions.

Up to now they had screened all sight of the thing in the cellar from the view of the watchers at upper windows on the opposite side of the road, while those on the street were being efficiently held back by the police. As they dispersed from the railing, however, a man who was gazing down with binoculars uttered a cry of alarm, and at once he was echoed by several other people.

"What is it? What is it?"

"Megaphone, please," Dougherty called. On being brought one from a nearby car, he set it to his mouth.

"Ladies and gentlemen, it's all over, please go on home or back to sleep!"

"But what is going on?" came answering shouts from a dozen throats.

"Nothing to get worked up about! We've just found a—uh—an unusual phosphorescent fungus! The sort of thing that makes rotten wood glow in the dark. It appears to be confined to this one house, luckily."

"What the hell do the police have to do with fungi?" the man with the binoculars bellowed.

"Ah . . ." Thinking fast on his feet, Dougherty said, "Well, there was an alarm over possible damage to the floors and joists. An old lady apparently thought the house was about to fall down!"

He added, "But we've sent for experts to look the place over, so don't worry!"

Grumbling, but convinced by the sincere ring of his lies, people responded by drifting away or closing their windows and returning to bed.

"Thank heaven it worked," Dougherty muttered, giving back the megaphone. "Right, let's move indoors like you suggested. It may help if we get off the street."

Someone had apparently taken Argyle away; at any rate he was no longer in the hall. Bella, though, and the constable, were still in the living room, the latter trying to control his nausea as Tom Gospell studied the parasite on Bella's back with the borrowed magnifying glass, occasionally jabbing at it with the end of his pen.

"Find anything?" he inquired as the others entered.

"Find anything?" Nick echoed. "Obviously you haven't been outside!"

Tom straightened. "No, I was going to come with you, but I remembered about the old lady upstairs—she's OK, just a bit overwrought—and when I came back down I decided to compare this with the thing I removed from Sally's back." He gestured at the jar, on an occasional table.

"You can look at that later. Go take a look at the adult version!" Nick grunted.

Tom blinked. "You mean"—pointing at Bella—"this isn't the adult?"

"No, that's the juvenile stage," Sally sighed, dropping into an armchair and shivering worse than ever. "Or to be more exact it's the unintermediated reproductive phase. The one in the cellar is the mediated phase. Incidentally, I should have stressed that even immature specimens are dangerous. By now there probably are several others, and they'll have to be located and disposed of, too."

Looking blank, Tom marched out to see for himself.

There was a gas-fire in here. Nick lighted it and Sally stretched grateful hands toward the flame. Rubbing his chin, Dougherty stared at Bella.

"Soon as the doctor comes back I'm going to find out if he can rouse her," he muttered. "I have a lot of questions to ask. . . . Well, for the time being I'll make do with you, young woman." Rounding on Sally. "You seem to know a hell of a lot that other people don't. When did you find out about the thing in the basement, and why didn't you report it to somebody?"

Sally just looked at him. Nick said swiftly, "What chance would she have had if she'd walked into a local police station and said, 'There are alien creatures at 5 Mamble Row'? Would anybody investigate that wild a story?"

"As a matter of fact . . ." Dougherty looked lugubrious. "You're right. Nobody would have called around even if the yarn were a lot less way-out than that. When Covert Squad puts a place under surveillance, we like to ask the uniform branch to steer clear unless it's unavoidable. People stop acting—uh—naturally when they think the fuzz are about." He hesitated. "But . . . oh, damn it! From another planet alien creatures—how the hell do you *know?*"

Before Nick or Sally could answer, Tom came back into the room, mopping his face.

"It's fantastic!" he muttered. "Never saw anything like it. Hey, what's happening to Bella?"

He pointed. The others turned. None of them had paid Bella attention for the past few minutes. Now the parasite she wore was withdrawing, though not as Alfred's had done, in a mess of blood and ichor, but leaving a clean hole behind sealed with some transparent membrane. The body of the parasite was condensing into a ball, like a giant unwholesome berry, or perhaps more as though a tight net were being closed around it, puckering its surface into hexagonal bulges.

Sally jumped to her feet.

"Oh, no!" she breathed. "I thought it must be through with its current cycle, but they must have saved one for Clyde. Tom, is there any more of the stuff that killed Alfred's?"

"Pethedrine? No, there was just the one vial."

"Anything chemically similar? I didn't know it worked so well, but— No, too late. Someone rescue Mrs. Ramsay! The rest of you, out of here fast *before the house blows up!*"

She almost screamed the last few words. Dazed, the others stared at her.

"Hurry!" she insisted. "For pity's sake! The Yem have three reproductive modes, not just two. The third is the projectile mode, and that thing is just going into it, and when a full-sized specimen bursts it can launch its spawn at greater-than-escape velocity. How the hell do you think Yem got here in the first place? Clear the street! Tell everybody to take cover! Even one that size can go off like a thousand-pound bomb!"

XX

And still they didn't react, apart from Nick, but gazed blankly by turns at Sally and at the parasite, compressing now, becoming visibly smaller, the six-sided indentations on it deepening—until there was a sound like a handclap, but muffled, which made them jump.

"Look!" Sally cried, pointing at the jar in which Tom had placed the thing he had removed from her back. Suddenly it had become opaque, as though a fine dust had been sprayed evenly over its interior, and there was a large crack in the glass.

"What happened?" Tom said incredulously, making to pick it up.

"Don't touch it!" Sally snapped, with such force he obeyed by reflex. "It went into projectile mode—how often do I have to tell you? Deprived of a living host to carry it to a good spot for planting, it converted itself into spawn and compressed gas, the way this bigger one is doing. Even a thread of Yem-stuff, so small you needed a magnifying glass to locate it, can explode violently enough to crack a thick glass jar. *Now* maybe you'll believe me!"

"I already did!" Nick exclaimed. "Get out of the house, then, quickly! Clyde, come and bring Mrs. Ramsay out too!"

He rushed to the door. Bewildered, but willing enough, Clyde followed him as he raced up the stairs three at a time.

Mrs. Ramsay screamed again as her door was flung open by two apparent madmen; in company with a woman police constable who must have arrived while Nick and Clyde had all their attention on the thing in the cellar, she was sipping a cup of hot tea and trembling.

"Out!" Nick exclaimed. "There's going to be an explosion!"

The policewoman rose uncertainly to her feet, while Mrs. Ramsay cowered in her chair. "I saw what they did to Mrs. Rowall!" she babbled. "Get 'em out of my room! Murderers, brutes, murderers!"

From outside came a huge bellowing voice; Dougherty had possessed himself of the megaphone again.

"Attention, attention! Get under cover, get under cover! There is a risk of a gas explosion! Keep away from windows, repeat *keep away from windows!* Stay behind a solid wall! Clear the street *at once,* repeat *at once!* Clear this street—take cover behind a solid wall—keep away from windows! Get back inside, you bloody fool! I just told you to keep away from windows and here you come sticking your stupid head out! *And* you over there! Go to the far side of your home, get away from this side of the house, *take cover!*"

And thunderous banging on the doors of the adjacent houses signaled the start of emergency evacuation.

The policewoman had just time to say, "But—"

Nick acted. He picked Mrs. Ramsay bodily out of her chair. Clyde pinioned her stiff legs, and between them they carried her clumsily down the stairs, the policewoman following in confusion.

As they rounded the last corner before reaching the hallway, Sally shouted from the front door, "Hurry, hurry! It's very nearly there!"

"Idiot! Why are you still in range? If you're killed what hope is there for other people?" Nick retorted, maneuvering their struggling burden down the last few steps.

Sally blanched, and turned tail at full pelt.

"Here, sir!" It was Hedger rushing up to lend a

hand. "Straight across the street, down behind the ambulance, OK? Sneak off behind parked cars."

"Got it!" Nick grunted, and they left the house, went directly over the road, and fell to the pavement in shelter of the ambulance as directed. Mrs. Ramsay seemed to have passed out.

"What is all this?" the policewoman demanded, staring both ways along Mamble Row. It was an extraordinary spectacle. The only person with his head up seemed to be Dougherty. He held a powerful police flashlight in one hand, the megaphone in the other, scanning the faces of the buildings from the far side of a parked police car. At that moment he spotted someone peering out, and bellowed a repetition of his earlier order to take cover. The head disappeared.

"There's Sally," Clyde whispered, pointing past Nick. "Right next to the inspector, see?"

Nick craned his neck.

"You get down and join her," Clyde muttered. "Mr. Hedger and me can look after Mrs. Ramsay."

"Thanks!" Nick muttered, and cautiously, scurrying with his head low, made his way along the pavement behind the close-parked cars to where Sally and Dougherty were tensely waiting.

He had just drawn close enough to hear Dougherty, bending down with an expression of annoyance, say, "If all this turns out to be pointless, young woman, you aren't half going to have some questions to answer!"

Blam!

It was as though a giant had coughed. It was as though the street were his body: all the people, all the cars, all the buildings, on his chest, so that they *shook*. An ear-shattering explosion was followed instantly by a rattle of falling glass, screams of alarm, what seemed like a hundred children starting to cry . . . and a menacing, horrible noise halfway between a hiss and a roar.

The blast-wave caught Nick by surprise. There was one last gap between the cars he must cross before joining Sally. He had been poised to dart past it; instead, he lost his balance and tumbled sideways, grazing his arm and banging his right knee. For a moment he could not see clearly. Blinking, he regained his vision and stared at Sally in mingled amazement and respect. To that, a second later, was added astonishment, for she was grinning from ear to ear.

"What's so funny?" he demanded, rising on hands and knees.

"Nothing's funny, but—oh, I know you don't believe in luck, but we've been *so* lucky! Must be because the Yem is new to Earth!"

Wiping his forehead, shuddering visibly at the narrow squeak he had because at the moment of the explosion he had happened to be bending down, Dougherty barked, "You say we've been lucky? Christ, it's wrecked the whole house and broken every window in the street!"

Closing the last yard between him and Sally, Nick winced. He had set his hand on a splinter of glass.

"But it went off early!" Sally cried. "It could have been twice as powerful, and what's more—well, see for yourself!" She stood up and pointed toward what was left of 5 Mamble Row.

Half the front of the house had fallen in a cascade of bricks and window-frames, splaying out over the sidewalk, the nearest cars, most of the roadway. And in this gap, torn out of the matched facades of the terrace like a tooth knocked out of a jaw, there was the source of the ominous hiss-roar noise.

There were flames. Leaping up, spreading far too fast even within the frame of such an old house. Huge sheets of red-yellow fire, peaking into pure white and dipping into roils of gray smoke.

Sally clutched at Nick, helped him to his feet regardless of the blood from his cut hand which dripped on her.

"Look!" she said again.

"I . . ." Dazed, Nick took in the scene, had to swallow and start over. "I lit the gas-fire."

"Right, right! Maybe it was the sudden rise in temperature that hastened the process, but anyhow when the thing exploded it shattered the main gas pipe and red-hot fragments from the fire must have set it alight and there's an end of the Yem!"

Nick stared at the ruined house, and understood what she meant. The explosion—he puzzled it out slowly, being on the verge of shock—had smashed the floor and ceiling of the room as well as the front wall. Something heavy had crashed into the cellar, broken open and gas pipe. The living room fire had been on long enough for the elements to be red-hot. Falling back, they had ignited the gas and now . . .

A sudden wail of sirens announced the approach of the fire brigade. Sally swung around to catch at Dougherty's arm.

"Inspector, you've got to let that cellar burn out, do you understand? Some varieties of Yem can resist fire—they secrete a special tough tegument—but that's too hot for any known specimen, so *let it burn!*"

Back in a more familiar world, faced with something much akin to an IRA bomb explosion, Dougherty glared at her.

"How the hell can you be so sure?"

"Because fire was the first weapon my people found to be useful against the Yem—"

Sally broke off in dismay, as though she had only heard the words issuing from her own lips after they had been spoken. Nick put his arm around her.

"Chief Inspector, surely you can at least tell the firemen that this house is past saving and the best they can do is damp down the houses to either side . . . ?" He bit his lip. "Got it! Dangerous chemicals liable to cause another explosion if you spray water on them! Oh, hell, make it uranium if you must, but tell them, tell them like Sally says!"

Dougherty took a deep breath, shrugged, and went to meet the puzzled firemen.

"I never thought he'd believe me," Sally breathed,

gazing after him. "Nick, you're wonderful!" She clasped his hand. "Oh, you're hurt!"

"Just a scratch," Nick grunted, wrapping a clean handkerchief around the cut. "But I don't think it was so much that I impressed Dougherty. It's more a question of his having been shaken to the roots of his mind. Incidentally . . ." He gestured in the direction of the blazing house.

"What?"

"That fire. It's not only destroying the adult—what did you call it?—Yem. It's also destroying the bodies of Alfred and Bella Rowall, along with their parasites. Right?"

Between them there was a dead pause, filled by shouts and the weeping of children and the noise of fire engines and the crackling of flames.

"Oh, Nick," Sally said at last in a small dead voice. "Oh, it can't go for nothing now, not when there may be scores of Yem at large carried God knows where by Bella's lodgers. . . ."

She collapsed against his shoulder and began to cry. He mechanically caressed her hair as he watched the fire flare and flicker, his mind growing blank from confusion and fatigue.

XXI

A pale-faced wall clock announced a dead time: four
A.M. They had sat now for so long in this drab corridor
at New Scotland Yard that Sally had dozed off against
Nick's shoulder. He envied her. He couldn't escape
from thinking about the implications of the night's
events.

*If they don't believe her, if there's no concrete proof
—just her word, mine, and Tom Gospell's—what will
happen?*

He wasn't sure what had become of Tom. He had
come here also, but in a following car along with Dr.
Argyle, and they hadn't seen him since they separated
in the foyer of the building. There had been reference
to calling in one of the top forensic pathologists; presumably Tom would be with him.

It was agonizing to have to guess and not be told.

At long last a man of about thirty who looked even
more tired than Nick felt put his head out of a nearby
door and called to them.

"Miss Ercott? Mr. Jenkins? I'm Sergeant Bray, Chief
Inspector Dougherty's assistant. Please come with me."

The office they were taken to bore the name *Deputy
Commander Harrison* on the door; they found
Dougherty there, and a red-eyed, red-cheeked man with
a bristling moustache whom he introduced as the senior
officer in the Covert Crime Squad. Harrison greeted
them frostily; he was clearly annoyed at being here at

this time of night. Having waved them to chairs and instructed Bray to find some coffee for them all, he sat back with a suspicious expression.

"I'm sorry to have kept you hanging around," he said. "But this has been a complex operation from the beginning, and suddenly to have it turn into a sort of lunatic dream is—to put it mildly—disconcerting. According to Chief Inspector Dougherty, what caused the explosion at Mamble Row was not a bomb but a kind of cancer on Mrs. Rowall's back, and he says you, Miss Ercott, gave advance warning and seemed to know far more about what was going on than anybody else. I find it very hard to take this seriously, you know. Excuse my being candid, but on the one hand I never heard of any growth on a person's back or anywhere else which could destroy a house like a well-placed charge of gelignite, and on the other, if my information is correct, you've forgotten everything about yourself bar your name and age. I'm doing my utmost to credit Dougherty's story because I know him for a capable officer and a good detective, but—well!"

Sally, not fully awake yet, rubbed her eyes, stifled a yawn, muttered an apology . . . and suddenly looked startled. She said, "I—I do know who I am! Since I explained everything to Mr. Dougherty, it's started to come back. It's as though my mind had been charged with data so important for the survival of mankind that everything else had to take second place."

She clenched her fists with excitement, her eyes shining.

"Wonderful! I remember that I'm Sally Jasmine Ercott of 19 Pebble Walk, Bristol, and I'm a research assistant for a technical book publisher, and I came to London for a weekend outing because . . . because . . ." She had to swallow hard. "A man I was fond of had just told me he'd decided to marry someone else, and—so on." She gave a wan smile. "Very likely neither my friends nor my family were inclined to look for me even when I stayed away for weeks. The same goes for my boss, because he—well, he was the man in question. They would all have known what a blow it was for me."

"This is beyond a joke," Harrison said, glaring at Dougherty, who was wearily shaking his head. "Putting it bluntly, I think you've taken leave of your senses. First you try to claim that the house was blown up by a cancer—then you ascribe the disappearance of these people we're searching for to a creature from some other planet—now, when I'm half convinced and willing to listen to what this girl has to say, it turns out she isn't amnesiac after all."

"But, sir—" Dougherty began. Harrison gestured at him to be quiet.

"I've had enough of this," he said. "I'm going back to bed. Dougherty, you're suspended from duty until further notice. Miss Ercott had better be examined by a doctor more competent than either Argyle or this fellow Gospell, and as for you, Mr. Jenkins, I think before you go home you'd better give us a written statement concerning your presence in the Rowalls' house. Where's the other man, by the way—this Clyde West?" he added to Dougherty.

Sighing: "Prior's been taking a statement from him, trying to get every detail he could about the way the Rowalls behaved toward their lodgers. When Mrs. Ramsay recovers I plan to do the same for her—but I was forgetting." Dougherty glared at his superior. "You just suspended me, didn't you? Well, I think that's the last bloody straw. I'll appeal to—"

The door burst open, cutting off his words. A man with a thin, sharp face, prominent teeth, and piercing eyes, marched toward Harrison's desk. And in his wake, a vast yawn parting his beard: Tom Gospell, carrying a glass dish with its lid secured in place by adhesive tape.

"Dr. Blatcham!" Harrison exclaimed. "What do you mean by barging in like this?"

"Barging in?" the intruder said, blinking. "Heaven's name, man, do you expect me to stand on ceremony when I have literally *world-shaking news?*" He planted his fists on the front of Harrison's desk. "I've been examining this fellow Argyle, trying to make sense of the growth on his back in conjunction with Dr. Gospell here, and he's run out of data but he claims that this young lady—you are Miss Ercott, I suppose? How do you do? I'm Gerald Blatcham and I'm a forensic pathologist as you've probably guessed. Where was I? Oh, yes. Dr. Gospell said if I wanted to know more I'd have to ask you."

"Argyle too?" Dougherty said, starting from his chair.

"We came here in the same car," Tom said, depositing his large glass dish on a vacant corner of Harrison's desk. "As soon as he realized where he was being taken, he went wild and tried to beat the driver over the head. I—uh—did a rather unprofessional thing, I'm afraid, and hit him to quiet him down. Whether by God or by guess, I aimed at the small of his back. My first sort of sank in, as though I'd punched a bagful of water, and so I suggested we strip him and look him over. And—yes, he has a growth on his back with extensions into the spine, just like the Rowalls."

"Not 'just like,'" Sally corrected. "That must be— what would you call it in English? Oh, perhaps the worker phase, worker in the sense of worker-bee. It doesn't breed, it only controls. I'd expect it to be yellowish rather than gray-green."

There was a moment of stunned silence. Then Blatcham exploded, "You mean you saw it?"

"Saw it?" Sally shook her head. "What reason did I have to be that fond of Richard Argyle?"

"Just a second," Dougherty said. "Dr. Blatcham, this —this growth on Argyle: it *is* yellow?"

"Yellowish. A sort of pus-color," Tom said.

Dougherty rounded on Harrison in triumph. "There! How could Miss Ercott have known that?"

"But it isn't yellow at all," Harrison muttered, staring at the dish Tom had set on his desk. "It's gray-green. I presume this is what you're talking about?"

"Hell, no," Tom sighed, reaching for and sitting in a vacant chair. "That's the one from Alfred Rowall, the one I accidentally killed. When orders were given to evacuate the house, I grabbed Argyle's medical bag for want of anything better and rolled the dead parasite in a corner torn off the bedsheet, and—there it is. In extended order, as it were, because Dr. Blatcham and I have been busy cutting it up."

"And I never saw aything remotely like it," Blatcham said with force. "I've dissected more dead bodies killed by more different causes than I care to try to count. I've been conducting post-mortem examinations for over a quarter of a century. I never ran across tissue resembling this stuff, and what's more it contains trace elements, particularly heavy metals, known to kill human beings in that concentration. It's unprecedented. I can't account for its existence. All I can say is that It's no kind of cancer. Containing the chemicals it does, it could not arise from malfunction of a human metabolism."

Nick was leaning forward intently. He said now, "You're saying it's unlike anything on Earth, aren't you?"

"I'm not sure I can go as far as that, but . . ." Blatcham hesitated. "Well, it's certainly never come to my notice, and offhand I can't imagine how such a remarkable condition could fail to be reported in the literature."

"That's because it's very recent, I suspect," Nick said. "How long since it arrived, Sally? A year or two?"

Before she could reply, one of three phones on Harrison's desk rang. The commander picked it up, listened, handed the receiver to Dougherty.

Having exchanged a few brief comments, the latter reported, "Something very interesting turned up at Bella's place in Soho, behind a baseboard. A tin cashbox containing not only some drugs and syringes, as you might expect, but also a list of over fifty names and addresses. At least a dozen correspond with people known to have disappeared."

"Marvelous!" Nick exclaimed. "Sally, could they be the people Bella infected?"

She nodded, uttering a sigh of relief. "That's going to make it far easier to track down the places where they—uh—sowed their Yem. We must be about the second toughest species the Yem so far ran into. What they prefer is a primitive or at best barbarian society, with few internal communications and ideally a lot of intertribal hostility. That gives them a chance to get established before the native bipeds can fight back."

"Sorry to have been so long, sir," Bray said, re-entering with a tray of coffee cups. "Oh, excuse me! I didn't mean to interrupt."

"I think it may be as well that you did," Nick said. "Suppose we drink our coffee, and then let Sally tell the whole story in her own words."

Harrison glared at him. "I still don't know where you fit into this, Mr. Jenkins," he growled. "Well?"

"I'm the person with an unconventional mind who caught on to the fact that Sally's been seeing visions of life on other worlds. But that's about all I do know for certain. You let her speak for herself."

XXII

The essential point (Sally said) *is this. We don't inhabit a universe that's merely big. We inhabit a universe that's infinite. Consequently everything that can happen, will. Sooner or later. In our case it's happened sooner; that's all.*

A billion years ago the first Yem evolved on a world where there was a species of bisexual binocular biped remarkably like the ancestors of Terrestrial man.

Between the vast plantlike sedentary organisms of the Yem, which reaped the harvest of a huge ecological catchment area by virtue of sheer size, and the small nimble creatures which achieved the same end by a combination of numbers and mobility, such intense competition developed that the process of selection for intelligence was improbably accelerated.

For the bipeds, possibly the transition occurred when one of them first recognized a Yem seedling, lone survivor in the wake of a forest fire, and picked up the cooler end of a still-burning branch and drove it into the burrow where the young Yem had hidden hitherto in safety. For the Yem . . . well, perhaps at the moment when it evolved its third reproduction mode, later to become the primary mode.

Its ancestors spread by reproduction tendrils. These initially would have been like suckers, issuing from the central mass, driving a horny spike into the ground, sloughing off eventually from the parent when established. Some minor varieties employed adaptations of this technique: they let their tendrils, also spike-tipped, blow away on a fierce gale or fall into a river which lower down fanned into a calm delta full of rich silt.

Long before the fight for resources began, this method had proved insufficient and had been supplemented by the projectile mode, discovered on Earth by puffballs. When a bad season endured too long, when there was a great drought or when the Yem population of a given region exceeded a critical density and there was no free ground in reach of the suckers, instead of expanding the creature drew in on itself, converting much of its substance into spawn, the rest into compressed gas. Eventually it would explode, and scatter its offspring by the thousand over half a continent.

In itself that might have been adequate. But the apelike bipeds had a different response to environmental pressure. They moved to new territory, and having learned to recognize Yem seedlings, routed them out as soon as they were spotted. Only the most fortunate Yem escaped.

Among these fortunate Yem . . .

Suddenly, as evolutionary time is measured, those spiked tendrils no longer inched across the ground or blew on the wind or floated down a river. They lurked, waiting for an animal to pass and tread on or brush against them. At first contact they injected a chemical that dulled the nervous system. To start with, no doubt, it was a simple poison. The wounded animal would travel more or less far according to the dose received, but it would certainly drop dead in a few days, and the corpse would fertilize a Yem in a new location. Very often, since the creature's nervous system was deranged, this place was a long way from anybody who might recognize and kill the seedling while it was still at its most vulnerable.

In terms of the development of the bipeds, this discovery was made late by the Yem. Bipeds were the best vectors, but just as they had learned to recognize young Yem they now learned to avoid places where

Yem thorns might prick them. They had invented speech, the use of tools as well as fire, and domesticated several animals; they likewise started to cull from their herds all showing signs of Yemness and burn their corpses. In many areas they became so successful they bid fair to exterminate the Yem. Starved of animal carriers for its next generation, though, it could still revert to projectile mode.

Doing so, it turned the tables.

The bipeds fought on for a long while, but now they no longer knew where to be alert for Yem; they might crop up anywhere, even inside their own settled communities. They lost track of which sicknesses were curable and which induced Yem-lethargy. Ten thousand years—fifty thousand—a hundred thousand—half a million . . .

The Yem triumphed, and in the process learned to reason. Ultimately they achieved intelligence, but they never applied it to any other purpose than survival. First there was a choice between available spiked tendrils: this will kill the carrier quickly, it's a good year with much rain, use it; this will kill slowly, it's a poor year, better the slow thorn for the carrier will cover more ground before it dies.

Often the changes, the choice-points, were far subtler. Sensitive cells grew into organs of perception. It emerged that the bipeds were unable to detect such things as magnetic declivity or the presence of another of their kind to leeward unless the other uttered an audible cry. The Yem had always known when another of the species lay nearby. There were pheromones. Eventually it became possible to tell when an animal had already been claimed as a carrier, and no other spike was wasted on it.

Along these pathways the Yem approached intelligence.

It won the battle. The cost was high. The bipeds had eliminated every strain of Yem bar the one which combined animal-carrier propagation, the ability to revert to projectile mode, *and* embryonic powers of reason.

These were rare. So it was another half-million years before another and even fiercer battle was joined. The Yem entered into conflict not with mobile animals but with other versions of itself. Having grown efficient enough to exploit every climatic zone of its home planet, from tundra to equatorial desert, it inevitably found itself collectively constricted. By now there was a sort of language functioning between its dispersed segments, akin to the hormonal messages in an animal body. The communication grew more complex as ever more specimens of Yem clashed with each other, attempted an accommodation, failed in face of the ancient overriding command now inscribed very deeply in its genes: *reproduce at all cost, reproduce!*

That stage lasted a long time, but finally—

One specimen grew so vast, hindered at every turn by its rivals, trapped in a double bind because it could neither find room to propagate nor resist the primal urge to do so at whatever cost . . . that it shrank after centuries into projectile mode, and its explosion launched Yem-spawn toward the stars. It spent its substance in the most colossal orgasm of all time, and dispatched something of the order of a *trillion* Yem-spawn into space.

A great many, obviously, died. A great many landed on barren asteroids or fell into the gravity-well of a giant planet. Few or none fell into the corona of a sun; they were so light, these fragments of the Yem, that they could ride the radiation-wind from star to star.

A handful, a few billion, did so, and drifted . . . and drifted . . . and drifted . . . and a few thousand entered a solar system whose sun shone on a planet not unlike the one where they had been spawned . . . and a few *hundred* settled to the ground. (This was millennia later, but no matter.)

There the Yem achieved success. There was a vastly varied fauna; the complex of chemical interactions proved tolerable; another million years went by, and the Yem, now greatly altered but more intelligent than ever, pondered the mystery of their evolution. They drew the correct conclusion: they must be foreign to this planet. Therefore they had once sown spawn into space. Therefore they might do the same again. Applying, as always, their intelligence solely to the problem of reproduction, they found ways and means.

And repeated the process. And again, and again. Each planetary generation, as it were, refined the technique. Instead of merely riding the radiation-wind the spawn became able to clutch (somehow) at wrinkles in the fabric of space; they could be directed toward a promising nearby star. It was possible that by now certain Yem had launched offspring clear out of the galaxy; however, that was a problem which might be postponed for another billion years. What was certain was that Yem had established themselves on literally thousands of habitable planets, every time selecting the native species nearest to the one on which it had earliest learned to prey: a binocular bisexual biped, not necessarily mammalian or warm-blooded or civilized or even intelligent, but having a—a cast of mind, an orientation, a collective personality, so to speak, much resembling the original quarry.

About the third or fourth generation, however—using "generation" in terms of the Yem's evolution on one planet to the point where it rediscovered space-seeding—occurred the first setback for its expansion. Never before had Yem-spawn been systematically trapped and destroyed.

We came on them—

"Now just a minute!" Harrison burst out. "What the hell do you mean, 'we'? I've sat here for the best part of an hour listening to you talk rubbish, and—"

"Rubbish?" Nick exploded, leaping to his feet. "You ask Dr. Blatcham and Dr. Gospell if it's rubbish! Well?" He rounded to them. "Well?"

Blatcham said apologetically, "I don't really feel qualified to—"

"Come off it!" Tom Gospell barked. "You already said you never saw or heard of anything like a Yem before. Well, it's a big universe! Room for anything to come here from anywhere else!"

Blatcham hesitated. "Oh, damn! I wish this could have happened to anybody other than me. . . . But you're right, obviously. Commander"—turning to Harrison—"my colleague has an excellent point. Faced with something we are unfamiliar with, and what's so far a logical account of the way it might have arisen, I'm obliged to say I want to hear more."

Harrison threw his hands in the air and fell back in his chair.

"OK, go on, then! But I won't promise to believe you."

"I'd nearly finished," Sally said. "I was going to say: we were the first species to find the Yem before the Yem found us. We— Oh!" A great light seemed to dawn. "I don't mean *we,* human beings from Earth, if that's what's confusing you. I mean *we,* human beings from . . . Just a second." She frowned and gazed into nowhere. "Not exactly human beings. A people with two arms, two legs, two eyes—come to that, two sexes —in other words an ideal target for the Yem even though since we were very tall, very lean and angular, and had scales rather than hair, I suspect we were probably also cold-blooded, what here would be called reptilian. What drove a reptile ahead so fast it evolved intelligence greater than Terrestrial man's, I don't know. I—" Seeming a little giddy, she put her hand to head, and Harrison erupted again.

"Oh, hell, woman, this whole yarn is absurd!"

"Not at all!" Nick said. "It is not ridiculous, it makes excellent sense and this girl obviously knows more about modern science than you do. So far I haven't spotted one flaw in her argument, not a single one. Sally, go on. You were saying that these people managed to beat back the Yem—"

"It wasn't quite like that," Sally interrupted. "They did very well at first, because they'd left their home world in search of other creatures like themselves whom they could communicate with, and finding how many of their cousins, as it were, had been simply taken over by parasites interested exclusively in breeding . . . Ah, what happened in short was they realized the Yem had a head start. So they established an—uh—early warning system. And of course that's why I lost my memory."

XXIII

"Oh, wow," Nick said faintly. "Yes, it all fits!"

"I," Harrison said with deliberation, "am getting very tired of listening to your exercises in pure fantasy. I propose to—"

"Don't," Blatcham said unexpectedly. Harrison stared at him. The pathologist returned the stare with interest and visible annoyance by way of bonus.

"Sorry, Commander, but this yarn is more than just fantasy, in my opinion. Have you come up with any more rational explanation for all those disappearances from Mamble Row?"

Harrison swallowed hard, but was compelled to shake his head.

"Well, you may not regard this explanation as rational, but you can scarcely deny that it's logical. Dougherty here, and others of your own men, saw something growing in that cellar which didn't look like anything known on Earth, and you must admit they're trained detectives with an excellent eye for detail, otherwise they wouldn't be working with the Covert Squad. Agreed?"

Harrison flung both arms in the air. "OK, you win!" he muttered. "I don't have to like it, though."

"It was a real stroke of good fortune that you'd set a watch on the Rowall's place," Tom said. "They were just about to cart us away to a cell when Hedger intervened, and I'm glad I didn't have to explain what I was doing kneeling on Bella while Clyde tied her up to people who hadn't seen the adult Yem. . . . Hmm! Speaking of that police watch: Sally, that must be what you were referring to when you called us the second toughest opponent the Yem has met so far."

"Of course. In our society people can't simply vanish and donate their bodies to fertilize the Yem without someone taking notice. Even without the early warning I mentioned we might still have come out on top. But naturally it's far better this way."

Dougherty said, "It would help if you explained what you mean by 'early warning.' "

Sally bit her lip. "I've been putting that off because obviously these people must have been scientifically far ahead of us, and I don't think there are words to describe how it was done. I know what was done, though. They so arranged things that whenever and wherever in the galaxy a swarm of Yem-spawn entered the vicinity of an Earth-like world certain personality-types among the local biped species would . . ." She hesitated. "Ah, the word I want is 'resonate.' I can't possibly be the only human responding, but I may well have been the first to pass close to an adult Yem."

"What does this resonance involve?" Nick demanded.

"First, the sensitive person grows aware of danger and the need for action. Then there follows the nature of the danger, and finally the command to inform other people and enlist their help. It's all programmed. You were absolutely right to say that my finding you wasn't luck but necessity."

"Never mind that. Go on."

"A few years ago a wave of Yem reached the Solar System. Endowed with means of detecting the presence of a suitable host-species, they headed in our direction. One, we know, landed in a spot where it could settle and start to grow. Reflex attracts them to major centers of population, so we'll have to make inquiries in India, China, Japan, and so on, but the odds are all against more than one of them finding such an ideal place as the Rowall's basement. I call it ideal because of the owners' habits.

"Once established, the seedling needed only to implant thorns in Alfred and Bella to obtain control over their behavior and a great deal of useful information about the local species—us. It must have been only a few months before it formulated plans for the conquest of mankind."

"That's a bit hard to swallow," Dougherty objected.

"Why? Countless generations have elapsed since Yem poison was so crude it merely killed the host more or less slowly. You saw what happened when Tom removed from my back the threadlike thing Alfred's parasite had implanted. My mind was dulled by it. I couldn't summon the energy to speak even though I already knew everything I'm explaining now."

Dougherty whistled. "Yes, that's right. You seemed to pull yourself together within seconds."

"If it hadn't been removed, it would have assimilated my entire consciousness and infused my mind with the knowledge that if I didn't do as it wanted I would die horribly and my body would feed another infant Yem. Alfred and Bella may not have wanted to obey their Yem, but they had to. The same goes for Dr. Argyle."

"You talked of the Yem formulating plans," Blatcham said incredulously. "You mean they become intelligent all by themselves—that they inherit intelligence automatically?"

Sally looked puzzled. "No, not 'all by themselves.' They can, when they're obliged to make use of sub-intelligent vector animals, but in that case they have to reevolve through several generations. In a situation like what we have on Earth, they acquire knowledge from the nervous system of the host; I thought I'd made that clear. It saves time."

"But that's unbelievable!"

"Not really. Not if you think of it as a magnification of what happens when a queen bee, or a queen ant, founds a new hive or nest. Remember this process has been in train for a billion years."

Defeated in his turn, Blatcham slumped back in his chair.

"I was saying that the odds are all against another spore finding an equally favorable location. The nature of Bella's two businesses—not only the lodging house, whose tenants could convincingly pack up and go to another city or even overseas, but her trade as a prostitute with many clients in London only for a day or two—offered the immediate chance of dispersing its offspring over hundreds of miles. That's not a combination likely to be repeated in a hurry."

"What I can't understand," Harrison muttered, "is how Bella managed to continue. I mean after the description you gave me, Dougherty, of this hideous object on her back . . . !" He shuddered.

Tom said, "Sir, it's regrettably true that many men are attacted by deformity. In *Patterns of Psychosexual Infantilism* Stekel recorded the case of a man who couldn't achieve climax unless he was kissing a woman whose mouth tasted of pus and blood."

Dougherty chimed in, "Besides, most of her—uh—engagements required her to wear kinky gear: leather corsets, black rubber, high boots, that sort of thing."

"Which must have made it very easy to transfer spores to the customer's backs. If they were tied up, maybe blindfolded too . . ." Sally hesitated. "As to the lodgers, that would have been a different matter. I'd better explain about the Yem's modes of reproduction."

"You already did," Dougherty grunted. "One goes bang, one takes people over, one—"

"It's far more complicated than that, I'm afraid," Sally cut in. "The adult Yem can arise from any of the three phases, but the intermediated phase can reproduce directly into the same phase again, which is what happened with Alfred and Bella, and it's only the next host which dies to feed the offspring, except when the prime-generation host resists control, which is fairly rare. Both can also go into projectile mode when fertilized but frustrated; that happened with Bella's parasite. There's a short time each year when the adult version, the type in the cellar, reproduces directly, and either implants intermediated spores on vectors, as again was the case with Alfred and Bella, or else implants the nonreproductive phase, the worker phase: for example Argyle. This usually occurs in early spring." She gazed from one baffled face to another. "I'm sorry, I did warn you it was complicated. Nick, did you follow me?"

"Perfectly. So long as Alfred and Bella went on obeying the adult Yem, its reproduction was assured, and it would not have acquired new—ah—new slaves until next spring. If they'd rebelled they would have died like the regular victims. And whenever either a parasite or an adult version ready to reproduce can't find a suitable vector, it seeds itself on the wind."

"Exactly! And the worker phase, of course, is simply a nonfertile counterpart of the parasite stage."

"Yes, this worker phase . . ." Nick rubbed his chin, looking puzzled. "I don't quite see what it's *for*."

"It's a late refinement in the technique for the Yem," Sally said. "As a matter of fact it was contact with us which— Oh, blast. I didn't mean to say *us*, because now I have it quite straight in my mind that I'm quoting the galaxy-wide signal. Now and then the Yem have run into species too clever to be exploited in the traditional way, and that's more receptive to the warning that's being broadcast. So it's learned to create what might be termed a bodyguard. In the early stages there are few spores to spare for nonfertile parasites; getting established is the overriding priority. Later, of course, when the Yem can reproduce from several focuses of infection, it's a different matter. Then these controlled slaves protect the sites of their masters, beat off attack, keep watch for trespassers, and if the local bipeds learn to steer clear, go out raiding for victims from beyond the range of the Yem's chemical attractants. I told you about such a raid. This particular Yem showed exceptional brilliance in picking on a dishonest doctor. I doubt whether all Bella's customers wanted to be tied up, and I'm morally certain it must have been Argyle who supplied drugs to keep the difficult ones quiet."

Dougherty nodded.

"I thought you said Yem poison did that anyhow," Tom objected. "So why—?"

"But the Yem doesn't always have spores ready to use, it can't always be sure of getting them to the right place, and even though it secretes powerful pheromones that lure victims to it these are only strong in the spring breeding season. The Yem has crowded itself off countless planets by over successful breeding; it's deliberately limited its own collective capacity. Once a certain number of vectors are known to have been properly implanted, the supply of spores dwindles. There's an element of self-regulating feedback."

"Was it pheromones of this type which compelled you to enter the Rowalls' house?" Tom demanded.

Harrison brightened. "Ah, now we're getting down to the part I want to hear about!"

Sally gave a faint smile. "Well, I left Paddington Station and took my usual shortcut through Mamble Row to catch a bus for the West End without having to line up behind a hundred other people who'd got off the same train. I passed the Rowalls' house, the Yem sensed that here came someone sensitive to the warning signal, and—as you say—it lured me in. Or rather drove me.

"But I was already 'resonating.' I said I passed out. When I recovered, my memory was overlain by the content of the warning . . . which, come to think of it, logically must be labeled 'memory,' mustn't it? To prevent the recipient mistaking it for a delusion no matter how hard he or she tries."

"Having got you in the house," Nick said, "why didn't it simply instruct the Rowalls to make you the next carrier?"

"Because there's one other component built into the warning signal, the most astonishing part of all." Sally shook her head, seeming a trifle dazed. "I can't even pretend to explain how they worked this supreme trick, but—Well, the people who devised it arranged things so that every time a victim of the Yem dies aware of what's happening and in full possession of his or her normal faculties . . . that reinforces the signal. It was the only technique they could invent which gave any hope of eventually outstripping the explosive spread of the Yem from star to star."

Nick whistled. "Neat! You mean each victim acts as a relay booster, to make the signal louder in the zone of maximum danger?"

"And to imbue it with the nuances that will make it more comprehensible to the local species. Not every victim · does this—some, particularly on a newly-attacked planet, die in ignorance of the real situation. But the signal is amplified by all who die conscious of the true threat. So the Yem didn't dare kill me at once. It had to wait until malnutrition and Argyle's injections combined to satisfy me that the warning signal wasn't to be taken seriously and I'd simply gone out of my mind. I came near to that, you know."

"Why didn't they use something fierce like STP or LSD?" Tom demanded. "An overdose of a major hallucinogen would have been positively guaranteed to drive you crazy!"

"I think this is where I really was lucky." Sally shivered. "Because, as I said, the Yem gains knowledge of a new planet from its vectors. And it hit on Argyle, who'd almost been sent to jail for dealing in illegal drugs. No doubt his mind was full of overtones implying risk, danger, punishment. . . . If it hadn't been for that—*ugh!*"

XXIV

Nick said thoughtfully, "So each of your visions was a sort of chapter heading within the total message."

"Right! The one which drove me out of the house and into your car was the most powerful because the most crucial. It stated that the Yem exists and preys on people like us."

"And the one with the four-armed barbarians?"

"It can take over control of humanoid beings, turn them against one another, exploit conflicts between them to make them serve the Yem's purposes and not their own."

"And the bit where you were a bride?"

"The Yem want only one kind of sacrifice. It's no good trying to buy them off, even with your most beautiful, most precious, most irreplaceable possessions. You can't placate them, so it's useless to worship them in the hope of softening the blow."

"And the bit on the planet of the double star?"

"The Yem can reduce the proudest race to the most revolting practices, can drag a once-civilized people back to savagery on the road to ultimate extinction."

"I notice you sometimes say 'the Yem is' and sometimes 'the Yem are.' Is there a reason?"

"Of course. It's because they're alien from us. They are neither a single organism nor yet are they individuals. *The Yem* is a species working with absolute unqualified determination toward one unique goal, neither possessed of a unified consciousness nor capable of achieving separate identities. What we really need is a new pronoun. . . ." She hesitated.

"On top of those I had one more vision, the most recent, the one which completed the message. It told me that somewhere, at some time, a girl very much like me, even though she was green and tall and covered in scales, was content to die at a lonely watch-post between the stars in the hope of saving cousins she had never met from conquest by the Yem."

The last words were spoken with such intensity of sadness that for a while the rest of them sat silent and unmoving.

At last Harrison stirred.

"Ah, well. I must have the courage of Dr. Blatcham's convictions, I suppose. It's true I set up this operation to trace the people who disappeared after lodging with or—ah—patronizing Bella Rowall. If the only course open to me is to put Miss Ercott next to all the high-powered scientists I can find, I'd better do it. I'm simply not qualified to cope with this.

"But that's for later. At present I'm too tired to listen to another word. Bray, find some cars and get these people home. And see to the other fellow, West."

"He can't go home," Sally said. "The house burned down."

"I'll put him up," Tom sighed. "I have a couch he can use. And I must phone my partner and ask if he can handle my morning patients, and—oh, yes. One other thing." He looked lugubriously at Dougherty.

"Chief Inspector, quite a lot of 5 Mamble Row fell on my car. It was insured, but . . . well, can I cite you as a reference to save having to explain that it was wrecked by a hostile alien being?"

Dougherty stared incredulously for a long moment. All of a sudden he burst out laughing. One by one the rest of them joined in, apart from Sally. When the near-hysterical merriment had died down, she said, "That's good. That's very good."

"What do you mean?" Nick said.

"That's why the Yem isn't going to turn us into

mindless vehicles for its children. It's too single-minded. It can't cope with people who find it so damn pompous that it's really rather funny. Come on, Nick. I think that's plenty for one night, don't you?"

Nick closed the door of his home and looked at Sally standing in the middle of the floor. She gave him a wan smile.

"You look worn out," she said. "I imagine I do, too. . . . But you're not just tired. You look thoughtful. Are you having as much trouble believing what I heard myself say as I am?"

"Yes, but that's not the whole problem," Nick said. "More, I'm wondering whether I shall ever again be more right than Tom Gospell."

Seeming to remember suddenly she was still unconventionally clad in the jacket Nick had loaned her at the Rowalls', she started to unbutton it. "What about Tom?" she prompted.

"Well, he issued me a stern warning not to get involved with a girl who was mentally deranged."

In the act of slipping off the jacket, she froze and stared at him in horror. "Is that what you think? Because if it is you can damn well—"

"Cool it, cool it," Nick sighed. "I said *I* was more right than Tom, and for the first time ever. I told you, he's a common-sensical type and I rely on him to restore my sense of perspective. For once I, with my warped mind and cockeyed view of the world, turned out to be on the right track when he was still being levelheaded and down-to-Earth. Yes, Sally, I do believe you. I believe everything you've said including the bits you don't believe yourself. Is that clear?"

She hesitated one second longer, then tossed the jacket at him, grinning.

"Perfectly clear. And I'm delighted."

"Mutual. May I offer my lady half a bed?"

"Yes, please. But even if you have the energy to proceed past that point, I promise you, I don't."

"That's fine by me. There's always tomorrow, isn't there?"

She was unzipping her borrowed jeans, and again paused in mid-movement, this time to scrutinize him from head to foot.

"I hope very much," she said at length, "there will also be the day after tomorrow, and the day after as well. And you know something very weird?"

"Several things, most of which you told me."

She chuckled and stepped out of the jeans.

"I didn't mean that. I meant something which I don't suppose I ever—cancel that, because my memory is coming back in full spate and so I know I never had it happen to me before. Here I am going to bed with you, and it's not because you buttered me up or I felt inclined for a bit of sex or anything like that. It's because you did something for me, me as a person, which nobody else in my life has ever done. You took me at my word when I thought I couldn't even trust my own sanity. Nick, I love you. I don't know you at all, but *damn* it, even if we never meet again I shall love you as long as I live."

Warm sun lit the room, soft hair brushed his cheek, and his hand rested on smooth skin. Wonderful! Nick was preparing to waken Sally in the nicest possible fashion when the phone rang.

Swearing, he grabbed his glasses, found the receiver, said in an ill-tempered tone, "Yes . . . ? Who . . . ? Oh, Clyde! Sorry, you woke me up. . . . *What?* Oh, that's fantastic! Are you sure . . . ? Thanks a million for letting me know. I'd begun to think it was all a bad dream."

He cradled the phone. Smiling, Sally rolled over and blinked a question at him.

"That was Clyde. Apparently Blatcham rang Tom's place a few minutes ago and Tom departed hell-for-leather. Would you believe they want him to look at what they think may be the first of the Yem?"

She sat up in delight and disbelief. "Never! How? Where?"

"Down in Cornwall, in the mouth of a disused tin mine, about a mile from the home of one of the people listed as clients in that cashbox they found in Bella's room. They've discovered a half-decayed corpse and a plant which a local naturalist claims he never saw before."

"Fantastic! Wonderful! Goodness, they must have moved fast."

"Not especially," Nick countered wryly, glancing at his watch. "We've slept away the entire morning, you know."

"In a good cause," she said, lying down again. "Shall we make it even better before we get up?"

"Yes please!"

Upon which the phone rang again. Nick swore.

"Sorry, should have taken it off the hook. . . . *Yes?*"

"Deputy Commander Harrison, Mr. Jenkins. I apologize for bothering you, but—uh—is Miss Ercott there?"

Blinking rather foolishly, Nick handed Sally the phone.

"It's for you!"

She listened for a while, sighed, said, "OK!" And replaced the receiver.

"Oh, dear. They want me at Scotland Yard. He's called together a group of biologists, and he's sending a car in half an hour."

"Half an hour! You could have held out for a *whole* hour. . . . Oh, well. I suppose logically speaking saving the world does take precedence. And there is always tomorrow, thanks to you."

He brushed her lips with a kiss and went to make some brunch.

☐ **POLYMATH by John Brunner.** Planet-builders dare not fail! (#UQ1089—95¢)

☐ **FROM THIS DAY FORWARD by John Brunner.** The many worlds of John Brunner revealing his talent for sf prediction. (#UQ1072—95¢)

☐ **THE WRONG END OF TIME by John Brunner.** A divided world faces the arrival of an alien warcraft off Pluto. (#UQ1061—95¢)

☐ **THE 1974 ANNUAL WORLD'S BEST SF.** The authentic "World's Best" selection of the year, featuring Sheckley, Ellison, Eklund, Pohl, etc. (#UY1109—$1.25)

☐ **HUNTERS OF GOR by John Norman.** The eighth novel of the fabulous saga of Tarl Cabot on Earth's orbital twin. (#UW1102—$1.50)

☐ **THE BURROWERS BENEATH by Brian Lumley.** A Lovecraftian novel of the men who dared disturb the Earth's subterranean masters. (#UQ1096—95¢)

☐ **MINDSHIP by Gerard Conway.** The different way of space flight required a mental cork for a cosmic bottle. (#UQ1095—95¢)

☐ **MIDSUMMER CENTURY by James Blish.** Thrust into the twilight of mankind, he shared a body with an enemy. (#UQ1094—95¢)

DAW BOOKS are represented by the publishers of Signet and Mentor Books, THE NEW AMERICAN LIBRARY, INC.

THE NEW AMERICAN LIBRARY, INC.,
P.O. Box 999, Bergenfield, New Jersey 07621

Please send me the DAW BOOKS I have checked above. I am enclosing
$_____(check or money order—no currency or C.O.D.'s).
Please include the list price plus 25¢ a copy to cover mailing costs.

Name_____

Address_____

City_____State_____Zip Code_____
Please allow at least 3 weeks for delivery